M000210683

THE
PRACTICE
—— OF ——
WITCHCRAFT
TODAY

THE
PRACTICE
——OF——
WITCHCRAFT
TODAY

An Introduction
——to——
Beliefs and Rituals

ROBIN SKELTON

A Citadel Press Book
Published by Carol Publishing Group

Carol Publishing Group Edition, 1995

Published by arrangement with Press Porcépic Limited.

A Citadel Press Book
Published by Carol Publishing Group
Citadel Press is a registered trademark of Carol Communications, Inc.

Editorial Offices: 600 Madison Avenue, New York, NY 10022
Sales & Distribution Offices: 120 Enterprise Avenue, Secaucus, NJ 07094

Queries regarding rights and permissions should be addressed to:
Carol Publishing Group, 600 Madison Avenue, New York, NY 10022

Manufactured in the United States of America
ISBN 0-8065-1674-7

10 9 8 7 6 5 4 3 2 1

Carol Publishing Group books are available at special discounts for bulk purchases, sales promotions, fund raising, or educational purposes. Special editions can also be created to specifications. For details contact: Special Sales Department, Carol Publishing Group, 120 Enterprise Ave., Secaucus, NJ 07094

The Cataloging-in-Publication Data for this title may be obtained from the Library of Congress.

Contents

Part II: Rituals and Celebrations

General Introduction

1   Commencement Rituals

Introduction
Making the Circle
Summoning Ritual
Ritual of the Powers
Ritual of the Watchers

Part III: Workbook

Introduction

Verbal Magic

Love Spells

1   To Find a Lover
2   To Bring a Lover
3   To Attract a Man or Woman
4   To Command Love
5   To Arouse Desire in a Woman
6   To Beckon a Lover
7   Spell with a Love Gift
8   Binding Spell, Using Spell Box
9   To Break the Bonds of Love
10 A Short Bond-Breaking Spell

Blessings

1   To Bless in All Ways
2   To Make a Small Plant Grow
3   To Accompany the Gathering of Vegetables
4   Blessing before Food
5   Blessing upon a Task
6   Blessing on Labour
7   Self-Blessing for Confidence
8   Invocatory Self-Blessing
9   Blessing for an Infant
10 Blessing for a Child
11 House Blessing

Banishings

1   House-Cleansing Spell
2   To Banish an Unwelcome Entity
3   Purification Spell

List of Figures

Preface

Although there are many existing books about witchcraft, the majority of them fail to give a clear picture of the Craft today. They concentrate attention upon the history of witchcraft and of the times of persecution in many instances, which is rather like devoting a book on Italy largely to a discussion of the Roman Empire. They spend a great deal of space documenting the various myths and beliefs about the Great Mother Goddess that have been important in the past, and thus obscure the central simplicities of the witchcraft credo. They enliven the proceedings by describing, and advocating, rituals which owe more to the sophisticated occultism of the nineteenth century than to the simple and direct ceremonies of the folk-religion in which the Craft has its roots. They advocate the use of spells which run counter to witchcraft ethics, such as death-curses and spells to gain personal power. Many, too, indulge in mere sensationalism and credulously accept the false evidence given by so-called witches under torture at the insistence, and at the dictation, of inquisitors.

Even the best of these productions – a number of them are listed in an appendix to this book – tend to present material of such complexity that the average reader cannot help but become confused. In this they imitate some of the occultists, such as Eliphas Levi, the complexity of whose instructions obliged his readers to seek further guidance and to pay well for personal instruction.

In this book I have attempted to describe the Craft, its beliefs and its practices, simply and directly. I have not given a long and sensational account of past tribulations, and I have not taken up space with long disquisitions on the history of goddess religions. I have presented rituals which are immediately intelligible and easy to memorize, and I have provided a spellbook which is both practical and in keeping with Craft beliefs. Those readers who wish to delve deeper into any matter I have discussed will find the annotated list of books for further reading a useful guide.

No single book could hope to deal satisfactorily with all the skills that witches learn. Some of these require, and have been given, books to themselves. I have not, therefore, dealt with the tarot, cheiromancy, herbalism, astrology, numerology or kabbalistic methods. These are, in any case, not central to witchcraft as such, though they are of importance to a good many witches. I have chosen not to go into the differences between the various Craft traditions, comparing Gardnerian with Alexandrian rituals, or explored in detail the debt some rituals owe to tantric practices or gnosticism. I have chosen, rather, to present what I perceive to be the essence of witchcraft, or 'Wicca' as it has come to be called, as it exists today. There is no orthodoxy in Wicca, and therefore a number of witches are certain to disagree with some of what I say, but such disagreements will, I think, be in terms of differing emphases and differing approaches to rituals; I do not believe that any true witch will disagree with my basic statements.

The statements and views presented in this book are as much the results of experience as of study. I began to study and practice witchcraft in the nineteen fifties and my devotion to, and the understanding of the craft developed steadily over the years. It was not until the seventies, however, that I encountered another witch, Jean Kozokari, and that my twenty years of work were rewarded by a formal initiation.

In making this book I have had the benefit of suggestions and critical comments from a number of fellow witches, and I am deeply grateful to them. It is, indeed, due to their encouragement, sometimes amounting to insistence, that this book has been written. They have felt, with me, that, at a time of growing religious conflict, not only within the Christian sects but also within Mahommedanism and the various faiths of India and Sri Lanka, it is important that a clear statement should be made about what, at least in its origins, may well be the oldest religion of them all

Part I

Answering the Questions

General Information

I have chosen to organize this section of the book in question-and-answer form, because in this way I can deal directly and straightforwardly with many of the questions that are asked about witchcraft, from the most simple and superstition-laden to the most searching. This has led to some duplication, for, inevitably, the answer to any one question is likely to include material that is essential to the answering of others. I have attempted to answer all the questions objectively, but my statements are obviously coloured by my own personal views. This is entirely proper, for there is no orthodoxy in witchcraft, and each witch has his or her own approach to the Craft.

1   What is a witch?

A witch is a person who follows the 'Old Religion', which he or she believes to predate the Judaic-Christian religion and which is nowadays called Wicca. Although some writers think the word 'Wicca' derives from the Old English verb *witan*, to know, and therefore means 'wisdom', this is not the case. It derives from the Indo-European root-word *weik*, which produced, eventually, the Old English word *wigle* (sorcery), the Old Norse word *wihl* (craftiness) and thence the English words guile and wile. Other related words are the Old High German *wihen* (to consecrate) and the Middle German word *wikken* (to predict). This leads eventually to the Old English *wicca* (witch) and *wiccian* (to perform sorcery). Thus the word witch contains within it notions of sorcery, cunning, holiness and prediction. The original Indo-European word *weik* had to do with magic and religion.

It must be realized, however, that the Old English word *Wicca* took on the meaning of sorcerer, of one who has dealings with evil spirits, at a time when the Christian Church was beginning to spread the idea that those who worshipped other gods than the Christian one and yet performed acts of healing or claimed to have spiritual power were certainly dealing with evil forces. An act of healing in the name of Christ was good; an act of healing in the name of any other power was bound to have been done by the agency of evil spirits.

'Wicca' may be the wrong word to use to describe the Old Religion, but it seems to have come to stay. 'Witch' may still be used as an abusive term, but then, once upon a time, so was the label Christian, and the term Jew is still, unhappily, used abusively in some circles.

2   What do witches believe?

A witch is a person who believes in the 'Old Religion' that is at present called Wicca. This religion is one that emphasizes the unity of the natural world and the spiritual powers that it possesses. Witches believe that all living things have 'soul' and spiritual power, and that the world is composed of a network of spiritual forces. These forces cause the rhythmic changes in all life, and the witch acknowledges these times of change by holding celebrations eight times a year.

In order to give form to these celebrations and to provide a sense of personal communication with the life-force that animates ourselves and our cosmos, witches, like members of other religions, personify the power they serve and worship. Wicca is a religion of the world of nature and of fertility. The worship of witches is therefore directed towards a Great Goddess, who, together with her male consort, rules the universe. This Goddess has appeared in many religions in man's history, and witches vary in the names they use for her. Many see her as being a goddess with three characters, that of the young maiden, that of the mother and that of the old woman who is wise and who is the layer-out of the dead. These three names may be Diana, the goddess of the spring, Selene, the moon goddess who creates the tides of the ocean and the menstrual tides, and Hecate, the goddess of the night. Other names for her include Isis (Egypt), Artemis, (Greece), Rhea (Crete), Ganga (India), Mokosh (the Ukraine), Brigid (Ireland). Her consort has fewer names in common use. Four of them are Cernunnos, Janicot, Herne and Karnayna. The Goddess is pictured as ruling from spring until autumn, and her consort throughout the late autumn and winter. Together they form the unity that in the Far East has been seen as the Yin and the Yang, the unity of feminine and masculine principles.

Some hereditary witches perceive the Goddess as quadruple rather then triple, and Hecate, the goddess of death and transition, as being seperate from the crone or old woman. For these witches the number four fits perfectly into a system of thought that lays stress upon the four elements of earth, air, fire and water, the four directions or points of the compass, and the four quarters of the moon.

There is no way in which one can summarize the beliefs of witches about the Goddess and her consort, for there is no orthodoxy in witchcraft. The names change from one group to another, and different groups emphasize different attributes of these powers. One can, however, easily state the central belief of all witches as regards human conduct. The Witches' Law, handed down through the generations, is "Do what ye will an (meaning 'provided that') ye harm no-one." To this is added the statement of principle, "Perfect Love, Perfect Trust". The law has also been expressed in the words "Love and do harm to none" and "Love, and do what you will under the law of love". The Old Religion is, indeed, a religion of love.

3   How old is the Old Religion?

Wicca is both the oldest of all religions and one of the youngest. The Goddess and her consort, the horned God, were worshipped in the Stone Age long before the construction of Stonehenge. Statues of the Goddess dating back to 25,000 BC have been discovered. They were plentiful in the Halfian period in Iraq around 3800 BC. The worship of the forces of nature, the belief that all living things have 'soul', appears to have been equally ancient, as does belief in the influence of the sun, moon and stars on the destiny of man, and the belief in the continuation of life after the body's death, and in some form of reincarnation. The latter may have stemmed originally from the belief that all living things are subject to the same natural laws, and the observation that all vegetation dies and is reborn. The view that death is the end, or that death is followed by eternal pleasure or eternal punishment in a heaven or hell, cannot be supported by observation of natural events. This being so, death should not be feared as likely to bring an eternity of punishment. Nor should it be welcomed as the bringer of eternal pleasure. Life continues, is perpetual and perpetual for all forms of life.

From these universal beginnings all later religions developed, some emphasizing the themes of survival after death, some emphasizing the themes of fertility and some retaining a belief in matriarchal society (as did a number of Celtic peoples). The majority, however, changed from worship of the Goddess to belief in a Father God, and from matrilineal to patrilineal society.

This change appears to have begun with the descent of Indo-European tribes upon the culture of the Middle East, which began around 2000 BC but which only gradually changed the religious attitudes and laws of the people. These tribes were patrilineal and patriarchal. The devotees of the Great Goddess were matrilineal and matriarchal. One cannot have a patrilineal society if the natural father of the child cannot be defined. Thus women were required, by new laws, to have sexual relations with one man only, the concept of female chastity before marriage was introduced, and the concept of bastardy. While some communities practised and continue to practise polygamy, polyandry was forbidden. Women who affirmed their devotion to the Goddess and celebrated her vitality and fecundity by sacramental acts of sex in the temple precincts were re-labelled prostitutes. Women became chattels, the personal property of men.

Other actions associated with the worship of the Great Goddess were also frowned upon, and in some places proscribed. As time proceeded, the dancing of men and women together was prohibited in some societies; the use of alcohol was frowned upon or forbidden; all music was obliged to be devoted to the tenets of a patriarchal and patrilineal religion. The celebration of the natural world by way of paintings was forbidden in some cultures: all paintings must be non-figurative in some Moslem societies; at one time in some Christian communities paintings were all to be devoted to religious Christian themes.

Nevertheless, the worship of the Goddess, in many different forms, remained the basic religion of rural communities in Europe for many centuries and at first was tolerated by the followers of the new religion of Christianity. In the eleventh century it was still common for there to be a 'pagan' altar in the church, which was almost invariably built on ground once used for pagan worship, and people would pay their respects to the pagan altar by the north door of the church as well as to the Christian altar in the east. Later, in the fourteenth century, the Church began to persecute witches; believers in the Old Religion were obliged to go 'underground', and the north doors of most churches were walled up and many of the north transepts transformed into Lady Chapels. From the middle of the fourteenth century to the middle of the twentieth, witchcraft was illegal in most countries of the Western world, and therefore the Craft became a secret knowledge passed down from generation to generation.

Even while witches were being hanged, drowned, burned and tortured, however, another tradition of 'magick' was being developed.

Beginning with alchemists who were part scientists and part magicians and who delved deeply into the mystical system of the kabbalah developed from the Jewish book of the Zohar, this tradition made use of names of power from the patriarchal Judaeo-Christian religion and was therefore considered relatively respectable. In the eighteenth and nineteenth centuries the increasing interest in folklore led to a conviction that old witch beliefs should not be lost, and when this interest was reinforced by the nineteenth century's fascination with spiritualism and mediums, the movement towards lifting the ban on Wicca had begun.

In 1921 Margaret Murray published *The Witch Cult in Western Europe*, which aroused both interest and controversy, and in 1933 she published *The God of the Witches*. Witchcraft had become a serious subject for research and study. As a consequence of this new mood of tolerance and curiosity, some witches began cautiously to show themselves. In 1951 the last laws against witchcraft were repealed in Great Britain, and Gerald Gardner (who had worked with traditional witches in the New Forest during the war, studied in the fields of anthropology and folklore in the East and already produced a historical novel on magical themes called *High Magic's Aid* in 1949) founded a Museum of Magic and Witchcraft on the Isle of Man. He also published *Witchcraft Today* and *The Meaning of Witchcraft*, which presented witchcraft beliefs, rituals and practices to the world.

Gardner's work influenced the Old Religion deeply. His rituals owed much to the occult and kabbalistic tradition. His admiration for the occultist Aleister Crowley led him to include some of Crowley's words in his rituals. He took material from the occult tradition and from the tantric tradition of India, as well as from those beliefs and practices he had learned from hereditary witches. It may well be that some of the implements now used by covens were first brought to Wicca by Gardner. I would suggest that the pentacle, being Judaic in origin and used by occultists, may have arrived in Wicca by way of Gardner.

After Gardner, many other covens and traditions surfaced, each one adding to, subtracting from and altering Wiccan practice, so that we now have not only Gardnerian but also Alexandrian witches (named after Alexander Saunders), Seax-Wicca (Raymond Buckland, USA) and a number of other covens with widely varied attitudes and emphases. I would instance the feminist Susan B. Anthony coven of California

(High Priestess Z. Budapest) as an example. Moreover, as soon as Wicca entered this revival, all the researches into the paranormal, all the studies in the rapidly growing field of parapsychology, were added unto it. Wicca is not a static but a developing religion. It makes use of new discoveries. It is, indeed, the oldest but also the youngest and one of the most forward-looking of religions.

4 What is magic?

S.L. Mathers, an occultist, defined magic as 'the science of the control of the secret forces of nature'. The word 'secret' may be taken as meaning that the 'forces', though natural, have not yet been thoroughly and systematically observed and categorized and that their mode of operation remains mysterious.

From another point of view, 'magic' might be defined as the power which causes an event or change to happen on command without any apparent physical cause or use of the known laws of nature. When we see something inexplicable that has clearly been intended to happen, we say 'It's magic!' or perhaps 'It's a miracle!' Stage illusionists are commonly known as magicians. The difference between stage magic and true magic is that in true magic what appears to happen has actually happened; in stage magic this is not the case.

We have labelled many events as magical in the past simply because the natural laws that caused them to occur had not yet been discovered or were not generally known. Hypnotism was regarded as magic, for example. So was magnetism. Until the twentieth century many folk regarded successful telepathic communication as acts of magic. Nowadays telepathy is one of many sometime 'magical' arts grouped together under the heading 'extra-sensory-perception', and the study of the 'magical' and of such phenomena as ghosts and poltergeists is dealt with by scholars of a new science labelled 'parapsychology'. No one has yet explained how 'magic' works, even though there is plenty of evidence provided by anthropologists to show that it does work. Witches can practise magic successfully but cannot explain the process, any more than philosophers can explain the operation of what is called 'thinking'. We know *how* magic works but we do not know *why* it works.

One current theory suggests that, as everything in the world possesses an energy field, and the human body possesses a very powerful one, an act of magic consists in focusing this electro-magnetic energy and transmitting it, often by way of a highly symbolic 'language'. This symbolic language appears to be of images which are transmitted either verbally or by mental pictures, accompanied by ritual acts which help the mind concentrate. This electro-magnetic energy may be similar to that emitted by the moon and stars, which astrologers believe affects the character, and therefore the destiny, of all creatures. It has been objected that the energy put out by the moon may be considerable but that such planets as Venus send out very weak impulses and are therefore ineffective, but one must recall that in medicine it is often the case that a small dose may be effective and a larger one either ineffective or counter-productive. One cannot measure effectiveness in terms of quantity in either medicine or mechanics.

The use of this energy, which has been called 'the Odic Force', or, simply, 'the Power', does not appear to be dependent upon any particular religious belief. Magic is not peculiar to witches. It has been used by practitioners of all religions, from the most ancient to the most modern. Sometimes the magical formulae are called prayers or hymns. Sometimes they are called spells or charms. They are to be found in Hinduism, Buddhism, Christianity, Mohammedanism and all other major religions. In most of these the magic formulae involve the use of the names of gods or spirits. These are regarded as ways of calling up and focusing the required energy. A strong belief in anything is productive of psychic energy. What we believe has reality for us; we are what we believe we are.

I have already described the witch's religion. This differs from other religions in believing that everyone possesses psychic power; it is not a kind of extra talent given to some few people as an act of divine (or diabolical) generosity. All human beings possess energy fields and therefore possess psychic power. Most of them use this power unconsciously or intuitively in their human relationships. A number, however, learn how to use it consciously and develop their abilities. I am not suggesting that, because everyone has power, everyone can be a witch, any more than I would suggest that everyone with feet can be a longdistance runner, or everyone with a larynx can become an opera star. We all share the same faculties and obey and use the same laws of nature, but in each one of us some faculties are more fully developed than others.

The magical power is not supernatural. It does not break natural laws. It is hypernatural.

Witches use faculties common to everyone. These are hard to describe, but one might summarize them under the general heading 'ESP'. We all have some telepathic abilities; witches simply have developed them and made them subject to the will rather than to chance. We all pick up 'vibrations' from places and people; witches have increased this ability. We all, whether we realize it or not, have the ability to perform psychic healing or faith healing; parents regularly do this for their children, and doctors' bedside manner and use of placebos are often as effective as their drugs. Where witches differ from other people is simply that they study and use these hypernatural faculties in a systematic fashion. The healing abilities of witches are well known and well documented, and their percipience in the use of Tarot cards is testified to by many people.

The witch's craft is not outside nature, not supernatural. Nevertheless, it remains mysterious. We can no more explain it than we can explain why some people are 'gifted' in one direction and others in another. And the 'magical' faculty, like all other human faculties, can be used for good or bad ends.

The difference between a witch's use of these powers and the use made by some others is simply that the witch works within the framework of a religion and an ethical discipline that prevents those powers being used irresponsibly or to harm.

5 What are black and white witchcraft?

These terms irritate witches enormously. Witches, who have utilized their legal right to freedom of religion and announced themselves believers in the Old Religion, are always being asked 'Are you a black or white witch?' The best answer I have heard is, 'If you are a Christian, are you a good or bad Christian?' The truth is simple. Acts of magic which run counter to the Wiccan credo of 'Love, and harm none' are wrong— they are indeed evil. Other acts are not. This was recognized before AD 500 by the Christian Church. Indeed, Constantine's law against witches was simply that witches who did evil things should be punished; others should not be harmed.

Unfortunately many catchpenny books about witchcraft, many books of spells, emphasize the sensational side of witchcraft and spend a great deal of time in explaining how to curse someone, how to get someone into one's power and how to satisfy sexual greed. Consequently many people think of witches as power-hungry and self-serving, and some of these people, who fancy the thought of possessing magical powers, decide they would like to be witches and even initiate themselves. They should be warned. There is a natural law that whatever magic one does returns upon the doer threefold. One may protect oneself somewhat, but only to a limited extent. One may achieve considerable power, but only for a time. The legend of Faust, though couched in Christian terms and in terms of occultism rather than witchcraft, can be read as the story of a self-indulgent, arrogant, malicious witch. Power itself does not corrupt, but the love of power, and the misuse of it, corrupts and destroys.

6 Do witches have a Bible?

There is no single authoritative text which commands the belief of all witches. As European witches began to be persecuted just about the time that writing and, later, printing began to be used by more than a few people, and since witches were, in those days and obviously, not taught writing by the main body of people who mastered the skill, the Christian priests and monks, the beliefs and practices of European witches were transmitted orally.

Some written material concerning other magical traditions and spellcraft does exist, notably the Atharva Veda of India, but this collection of spells and rituals is expressed in terms of the Hindu pantheon and in terms of Indian social customs. Fragments of spells, charms and rituals have survived from ancient Assyria and the early civilizations of the Middle East, and, of course, there is a good deal of important material to be found in Egyptian tombs and papyri, and in the Tibetan *Book of the Dead*. Most of this material is fragmentary, much largely unintelligible, and a great deal of it would have to be modified quite considerably to fit with Wiccan beliefs and traditions. The so-called 'Gospel of the Witches' given C.G. Leland by an Italian witch in the I880s is little more than a legend which tells how the Goddess, Aradia, came into being. Witches therefore do not have a Bible.

On the other hand, it could be said that witches have not one Bible but many, for every witch or group of witches possesses a 'Book of Shadows', which is a comprehensive setting-out of rituals, initiation ceremonies, invocations, incantations, spells, herbal lore and the various techniques that the witch or the coven uses. Some of this material is traditional and has been handed down from generation to generation. Some is produced as a result of research into, and modification of already published rituals from other cultures, or from the witches' own culture. Because of the overall belief in the Goddess and God, and the common understanding of the Craft and the sharing of fundamental symbolism, these Books of Shadows are often similar, but they are equally often different. A coven working in a desert will not use the same symbols as one working beside the sea; the natural forces of the area differ, not in essence but in degree and nomenclature. Moreover, each coven is likely to have its own bias: some covens devote themselves wholly to healing, for example; some are concerned largely with divination and with exorcism; some work naked and some clothed.

Another reason for lack of written material in the past was the traditional view that when a witch dies his or her Book of Shadows should be destroyed. This was, of course, a wise precaution in earlier days. The tradition has been also that all this material should be kept secret, and many Wiccan initiations still include an oath or vow of secrecy. Now that witches are no longer in danger of legal persecution, and now that a good deal of previously secret material has been published, it is no longer necessary to keep everything secret, and a number of Books of Shadows used by witches of today have been published. The curious researcher therefore may now consult several Books of Shadows, but even the most assiduous worker could not, by collating them, and abstracting all the points of agreement, reach an authoritative 'Bible' or even a Book of Common Prayer.

7 Do witches worship the Devil?

The answer is 'No.'

First, the Devil is a figure in Christian doctrine, and Wicca predates Christianity. Moreover, the figure of Satan, or the Devil, was almost entirely ignored by the Church until the sixth century AD, when it became politically wise to identify the horned consort of the Goddess as equivalent to the adversarial figure who is featured in Genesis and the Book of Job and who acts as a scrutineer of Christ's conscience in the forty days in the wilderness. (It was around this time also, incidentally, that the doctrine of reincarnation previously tolerated by the

Church was considered to be false, and the notion of man's having one life which resulted in eternal pleasure or eternal torment was emphasized.) The picture of the Devil as horned and goat-footed derives from the image of Pan and is nowhere found in the Bible. The word 'devil' may derive from the Sanscrit 'deva', meaning 'shining one', or even from the Latin 'deus', meaning 'god'. The gypsy name for God is Duvel. Old Nick, another name for the Devil, derives from the Norse god Nik.

In the times of persecution, witches often confessed to having had intercourse with the Devil, whom we now know to have been simply the leading male of the coven, who would sometimes wear a horned head-dress and a cloak of skins. The Devil has been credited with supervising many of the pleasures of ordinary folk. Dionysus and Cernunnos, in older religions, were patrons of beer and wine. Puritans considered alcohol the work of the Devil. They also considered dancing devilish: dance is an integral part of Wiccan celebrations. Indeed, the Christian Church in its various forms has credited the Devil with almost everything that takes man's mind away from considerations of guilt and consequent damnation, or asceticism and subsequent bliss. It is odd to reflect, however, that the Church has not invented a female Devil, although the Fall of Man in the Garden of Eden occurred as a consequence of Eve's original sin. Nevertheless, the figure of the Goddess remains, in Catholicism anyway, a most important image of divinity.

8 Are witches anti-Christian?

All witches revere the story of Jesus Christ and his gospel of love; although it is couched in the terminology of the patriarchal society into which he was born, and therefore makes use of concepts of monogamy and of monotheism which are not part of all witches' beliefs, his wisdom is awe-inspiring. Moreover, his miracles reveal him to have been an adept in the use of powers that all witches recognize and use in the service of their worship of love and the all-encompassing spirit.

The organizations which have grown up around Christ's teachings and which have so often denied them, or elaborated them in a fashion quite alien to his message, are another matter. It was not Christ but the Church that first stated that witches did not exist and that to believe in them was heresy, and then that witches did exist and that not to believe in them was heresy. It was not Christ but the Church that, after 500 years of tolerating, if not wholly accepting, belief in reincarnation, made belief in reincarnation a heresy. It was not Christ but the Church that decided that 'Thou shalt not kill' meant 'Thou shalt not kill anyone but heretics, murderers, thieves, witches, Mohammedans, heathens and anyone else the Church decides.' It was not Christ but the Church that invented the Inquisition and killed millions of Jews, gypsies and witches in Europe over a period of four centuries. It was not Christ but the Church that, in the sixth century, invented the horned, goat-footed Devil, who in the Gospels is simply the expression of an opposing point of view, the tempter, and a part of Christ's own internal debate in the wilderness.

Witches are not opposed to anyone practising whatever religion they find meaningful to them. They do not proselytize or attempt to convert people to the Old Religion. They believe that people, moving through many lives, must pass through many stages of understanding and must work out their own destinies. Help or advice or teaching will be given when asked for; it will not be imposed upon the unwilling.

If witches are opposed to anything, they are opposed to curtailment of human liberty of choice, to restrictive dogmas that damage and limit spiritual progress and to all that hurts or harms, for the keystone in the Wiccan 'Church' is 'harmony and freedom within love'.

9   What are sabbats?

Sabbats are the celebratory feasts held by groups of witches eight times during the year.

The four most important sabbats are held on 31 October, Hallowe'en, which is called Samhain; on Candlemas, 1 February, which the Irish called Imbolc or Oimelc and viewed as a feast for the quickening of the year; on May Eve, 30 April, Roodmas, which the Irish called Beltaine; and on Lammas, 1 August, which is the ancient feast of the Celtic sun god, Lugh, and called therefore Lughnasadh.

The other four sabbats are held on 21 December, which is the time of the winter solstice and the Norse feast of Yule, which the ancient Celts called Alban Arthan; on 21 March, the time of the spring equinox, which the druids called Alban Eilir; on 23 June, St John's Eve, or Midsummer Eve; and on 21 September, the time of the autumn equinox, which the druids called Alban Elfed. Witches also hold minor celebrations at the time of each full moon. These meetings are called esbats and are less formal occasions, though they are often used to work magic. Some covens also hold celebrations on other days of their choice.

What happens at any sabbat will depend upon the traditions and practices of the particular coven or covens involved. The feasts at the greater sabbats sometimes include more than one coven. Some activities are common to all sabbats, however. There will be feasting, music, dancing and drinking as well as the performance of rituals. Whenever possible, there will be a bonfire around which the participants will dance and through which, on some occasions (most usually midsummer), they will leap. Sabbats are the usual occasions for the marriage of witches to take place. These are called handfastings. A witch couple may also present their newborn child to the Goddess and the God in a ceremony of dedication and thanks. Future magical projects may be discussed, and some work may be done, but in general the sabbats are meetings for worship and celebration, except on special occasions.

In olden days the sabbats were also occasions for making love. Indeed Beltaine, 1 May, was regarded as the day for love-making, and the phallic maypole remains as a relic of those times. Children born as a result of love-making on May Day were often regarded as children of the God and given an appropriate name, such as Robinson— meaning the son of Robin, which was one name for the god of the woodland. A child conceived on Beltaine would be born on or just before 2 February, St Brigid's Day. This meant that the woman would be unable to work in the fields only during the winter, when there was no work to be done. Many folk-songs testify to the traditional notion of the 'merry month of May' as a time for creating children, and the spring season has always been regarded as the time for betrothals. It should also be noted that a child conceived on any sabbat would be born just before another sabbat, at which it could be dedicated to the service of the Goddess.

There is some disagreement over the word sabbat. It seems unlikely that it derived from the Jewish Sabbath, as Wicca pre-dates Judaism, and the Sabbath is after all a weekly feast. Doreen Valiente suggests that the word may be descended from the cry of 'Sabai' or 'Evoi Sabai' which was used by the devotees of Dionysus, one of whose names was Sabadius or Sabazius. Some old European names for the sabbat translate into English as 'the field of the goat'.

The sabbat in olden days is supposed to have been presided over by the male leader of the coven. Modern sabbats are usually presided over by the High Priestess or by the High Priest and High Priestess together.

The dances at the sabbat are various. Apart from the dance around the fire in a circle, which is almost universal, some groups enjoy other dances, both old folk-dances such as those of the morris dancers – many of which are magical and ritualistic in origin – and modern dances. Traditional folk-music may be played; so may other kinds of music, according to the tastes of the participants.

10   Do witches raise spirits?

Here we come across the difference between witchcraft and ritual magic, between the tradition of Wicca and the tradition of the occult.

The practitioner of the occult works within a circle, as do witches, but it is his or her intent to *evoke* spirits, who will appear to him outside the circle. The circle is intended as protection, for the occultist's aim is to dominate and command the spirits that have been raised. Whether these are indeed spirits external to the magician or controlled hallucinations originating in the unconscious of the operator, or maybe a little of both, remains a matter of doubt. The witch, alone or in a group, also works within a circle but does not *evoke* spirits. He or she *invokes* the Goddess, the God, the old powers, asking their presence within the circle, so that the power and will of the Goddess may become the power of the witch to perform magical acts and rituals. The basic difference could be stated simply thus: the magician uses the circle as a defence against spiritual powers; the witch uses the circle to welcome spiritual powers and become one with them. The magician *evokes* the powers; the witch *invokes* them.

There are other differences also. The occultist ritual magic most usually involves incantations that include the names of so-called angels and demons which are found in the Judaic and Christian traditions, and the names of the masculine gods of Judaism, Christianity and Mohammedanism are used. The magician does not, in fact, work in terms of the Old Religion at all.

Having said this, I must add that many witches do make use of some of the techniques and symbolic systems that were originally the province of magicians. They use the symbolic and mystical system of the kabbalah (Quabalah) which derives from a Jewish book, the Zohar, and practise the techniques of Notarikon and Gemetria as well as the system of numerology which also derives from Hebraic mysticism. Although the authoritative monotheism of Judaism and its codes of behaviour are unacceptable to followers of the Old Religion, some parts of the kabbalah – though not all – fit perfectly with traditional Wiccan belief and practice.

Witches are pragmatists. If techniques derived from other traditions prove effective and do not run counter to Wiccan belief, it is proper to use them. Thus many Wiccan rituals contain elements which historians perceive as deriving from Indian and Tibetan tantra, from Sufism, from North American Shamanism and so forth. A technical discovery is valuable, whoever discovers it. I must emphasize, however, that the witch uses the techniques in the service of the Old Religion, just as, let us say, a Christian doctor might utilize drugs which were discovered first by Indian shamans and used by them in the service of their religion.

11   Is witchcraft an occult tradition?

My own answer to this question is 'No', but the word 'occult' has, of recent years, been used as a general term descriptive of all magical traditions, so that it is necessary to clarify the situation and perhaps redefine some terms.

I have already outlined the religion of Wicca and its basic beliefs. Occultism is not a religion, as is Wicca. Indeed, there are occult traditions within several major religions. Western occultism may reasonably be said to have begun in Judaism, though the Judaic tradition was much affected by Chaldean and Babylonian and Egyptian magic. The centre of occultism is a belief in a world populated by many supernatural 'demons', 'angels' and 'spirits'. While Wicca believes that everything created has an 'energy field' which may be regarded as a 'spirit', it does not believe in any power unattached to the world of nature. The occultist practises ritual magic in order to summon up spirits or demons and command them to do the magician's bidding. The spirits summoned are regarded as external to the summoner. The magician makes a circle to keep spirits out and to control them; the witch makes a circle to bring spiritual power into it and to use that power.

The Western occultist often works in terms of the Jewish or Christian religion, summoning up the forces labelled by the Judaic writings as 'devils' or 'angels', these being ranked in elaborate hierarchies, each one with particular powers and attributes, and many also associated with a particular star, planet, metal or gemstone; almost none are related to plants or trees. Astrology plays a great part in occultism, and stems in all probability from Zoroastrianism. Witches do set considerable score by astrology, but not in terms of angels or demons.

Alchemy, which had its beginnings in Egypt and flowered in fourth-century Byzantium, and which later led to the science of chemistry, was an occult art/science dealing not merely with the transmutation of base metal to gold by physical means but with the manipulation of spiritual forces. Some alchemists were also reputed to be magicians and to have attempted (in the case of Dr. Dee, Elizabeth I's astrologer, supposedly with some success) to raise the Devil. Dee and his confreres did not worship the Devil; they wished to consult and command him to do their bidding. From this practice, of course, came the medieval story of Faust.

The procedures of the alchemist and the ritual magician were elaborate and were only for the wealthy who could afford to buy the equipment needed for rituals which invariably involved complex acts of protection from the somewhat recalcitrant powers called into service. Moreover, just as the angels were organized hierarchically, so were the various secret magical orders, every one of which, in the Western tradition, was male-dominated, and most of which permitted only male membership. There were several classes of membership, from neophyte to adept. Each step up the ladder was achieved by way of the study of rituals, symbolism and much arcane law. Each magician, in most cases, would be obliged to possess ritual clothing, more or less elaborate, and a number of other symbolic objects, including a sword, wand, black-handled knife, white-handled knife, cup or chalice, pentagram (sometimes on a cloth that could be spread out on the floor), smaller pentacle, wand, incense-burner and so forth. Rules were laid out for the materials to be used for these objects. Many had to be made by the magician himself. Some required particular precious and semi-precious stones.

This tradition led in many directions and produced a considerable number of secret societies, from the no longer particularly occult Masonic orders to the Order of the Golden Dawn. Some orders emphasized self-illumination. Some emphasized the gaining of power. Some, derived from the Christian tradition, decided that the rule of Satan was preferable to that of the Church, and various Satanic cults were organized. These orders (with the notable exception of the Masons and other secret societies which were really 'friendly associations' and did and continue to do much charitable work) were not concerned with the good of society. They did not practise healing, as does Wicca; nor did they have a tradition of herbalism. The sexual rituals and practices of Hindu tantrism crept into occultism in the late nineteenth century and deeply influenced Aleister Crowley who, in turn, influenced Gerald Gardner and therefore Gardnerian witchcraft.

The difference between Wicca and the occult tradition lies in more than their origins, their implements and their activities. There is a philosophical difference. The occult tradition separates humanity from nature, in accordance with the statement in Genesis 1:26: 'And God said, Let us make man in our own image, after our likeness: and let them have dominion over the fish of the sea, and over the fowl of the air, and over the cattle, and over all the earth, and over every creeping thing that creepeth upon the earth.' In verse 28 of the same chapter, man is told to: 'Be fruitful, and multiply, and replenish the earth, and subdue it.' Wicca takes the view that humanity should not 'subdue' the natural world but work in harmony with it, and that the rhythm of human life should be attuned to the rhythms of the natural world.

The occult tradition, with its lore of spirits, angels and demons and its belief in a complex system of hells and heavens does not pay much attention to the life in the world and on the earth. Wicca, believing that there are no hells or heavens in the occult sense but that life is perpetual and that each human creature, and perhaps all living things, may experience life on earth over and over again, is very much concerned with the quality of life on earth.

The occult tradition is essentially Manichean in its perception of a constant war between Good and Evil; Wicca does not see the universe in that fashion, believing rather that all the living things in the universe obey universal laws and are capable of actions which, from humanity's limited point of view, may be regarded as 'good' or 'bad' but which are not 'good' or 'bad' in themselves. These actions can be affected and altered both by the human will and by the operations of the natural world, by the rhythmic changes of seasons, the movements of stars and planets, and the influence of the spirits of place and of the spirits of all living things. The universe is a constantly changing interwoven web of energies; there is nothing static in it.

To the occultist, true mastery lies in dominance; to the witch, true mastery lies in understanding and working within the natural harmony. The occult tradition deals in that which is regarded as above and separate from the natural world, in the supernatural. The Old Religion does not believe in the supernatural.

12   What is a coven?

A coven is a group of members of the Craft who meet and work together. Traditionally a coven should consist of thirteen people. This really means that no coven should be bigger than that. The number thirteen is also symbolic. A popular superstition states that it is intended to parody the thirteen composed by Christ and the twelve disciples. This is nonsense. Witchcraft existed long before Christianity, as did the significance of the number thirteen. The Goddess is, in one of her guises, Diana the moon-goddess, and there are thirteen moons in the year. Indeed, the feast of Diana took place, in Roman times, on 13 August, which is now, in the Roman Church, the feast of the Assumption of the Virgin. Romulus, who founded Rome, had twelve companions; King Arthur, according to some sources, presided over twelve knights at his round table; the Emperor Charlemagne had twelve paladins to support him; Robin Hood's band, again in some versions only, consisted of twelve men and a maid. The British jury system lays it down that a man must be found innocent or guilty by 'twelve good men and true' and a presiding judge. Oddly, and perhaps irrelevantly, a 'baker's dozen' amounts to thirteen loaves.

In fact, however, many covens consist of fewer than thirteen people, and they certainly do not conform to one tradition which states that there should be six men, six women and a male leader. This may possibly derive from the Norse mythology which saw the god Odin as ruling over a group of six goddesses and six gods. Thirteen is also a practical number, for, just as in a study workshop or seminar, the larger the group, the less effective the communication between its members will be, so in witchcraft it is extremely hard to get a large number of people to share and project exactly the same emotion and intent.

All groups need an organization of some kind. Covens therefore are 'led' most commonly by a woman and a man, who are termed the Priestess (or High Priestess) and the High Priest. Some covens with an itch for antiquity name these Maid and Magister, Robin and Marian, or give other titles. The system is not, however, rigid. Indeed, the 'leaders' of a particular work or ritual may change from time to time, according to the situation. When a coven reaches the figure thirteen, one of the group is required to go and start another coven. This is usually an experienced person, often one who has served as High Priestess. A High Priestess or High Priest who has organized and brought several covens into being is sometimes called a Queen or King, but this is merely a term of honour and carries no additional authority or power.

The coven meets on all the sabbats and, less regularly, when the moon is full. It usually has a set meeting-place— it seems that in the past this was in the open air, on a moor or heath, though one wonders how they coped with inclement weather. These days some covens have rooms used only for meetings, and these are often called sanctuaries or chapels, but many meet in the members' houses. Most covens meet for study as well as for rituals and for making magic, and many have libraries from which members may borrow books. In any coven there are likely to be specialists in one or another aspect of the Craft, so that there is a 'resource person' to deal with any problem that crops up.

It is popularly supposed that witches meet in graveyards and dance around the tombstones. Most churches in Europe were built upon ground used for Wiccan gatherings, and so it became not unusual for witches to continue to use the ground around the churches for their meetings, which usually did involve dancing. The ground around churches, was not, however, used as graveyards in most countries until the seventeenth century, so the presence of graves has nothing to do with the witches' choice of churchyards as meeting-places. Places with high energy-levels are often chosen, such as standing circles and places where waters meet underground or rise up to make a spring or well. So-called 'holy wells' were often sites for gatherings.

Today some witches structure their covens more strictly than others. Some insist that witches should proceed through 'three degrees' of witchcraft, a notion almost certainly derived from the tradition of the occultists, with their emphasis upon hierarchical progression from

neophyte to adept. Some witches have established their groups as legal
'churches', largely for tax reasons and to give the group some social
standing and therefore protection. Some covens make a rigorous distinction between priests and priestesses and others who are regarded
as students or simply called worshippers. In general, however, the
structure of Wiccan society is simple and practical and involves no
class-distinctions. We are all sisters and brothers in the Craft, each
having our own particular specialities and abilities, and no one soul
being superior to any other.

Covens do not advertise their meetings. Witchcraft is a 'mystery
religion', and the public are not invited. Witches do not proselytise. It is
as difficult to receive an invitation to a working coven as to receive an
invitation to attend one of the potlatches (winter dance festivals) of the
Kwakiutl or Haida Indians of British Columbia, for theirs is also a
mystery religion. Nevertheless, sometimes one does find groups of
people who call themselves witches inviting the public to attend and
take part in rituals, usually for a fee. There have even been public
invitations to join covens. I find it difficult to believe that those who
organize such things are true members of the Old Religion.

13   Do witches perform sacrifices?

One of the accusations made against witches in the past was that
they killed unbaptized babies and sacrificed them to Satan. (The same
slander was used to vilify Jews and, sometimes, gypsies.) There is no
acceptable evidence in support of this accusation. Indeed, the only
evidence available is provided by those who, on encountering infanti-
cide, immediately stated that the killer was a witch.

Certainly, if we are to believe our earliest and most credulous
historians, the tribes of Celtic Britain in the druidic period did perform
human sacrifices. It has also been stated by Frazer in *The Golden Bough*,
and by Margaret Murray, that in the Old Religion the Divine King (or
his substitute) was ritually murdered after seven years' reign, King
William Rufus' death in the New Forest being adduced as certain proof
of this. Animal sacrifices occur in a great many cultures, of course, the
entrails being consulted for purposes of divination and the flesh pro-
viding the main course of a feast.

In order to get this subject into perspective, we must look at the
word 'sacrifice' itself. The word derives from the Latin *sacer* (holy) and

facere (to make). Something is made holy by giving it to the god, goddess or gods, and thus 'sacrifice' grew to mean giving something up, perhaps in hopes of reward, perhaps not.

Sacrifice involves destruction; the sacrificial object or creature is destroyed. But there is no such thing as absolute destruction, for life is perpetual; there is only transformation. Thus sacrificial destruction is really an act of transformation, a moving of the sacrifice from one plane of being to another. If this is done in order to 'make holy' the object or creature, no evil has been performed. We must here, however, consider the Witch's Law, 'Do what thou wilt, and harm no one.' We must not send a living creature on to another plane of existence without most careful consideration of all aspects of the matter. No human creature should be killed without his or her wholehearted assent, and where that assent cannot be given, as is the case with the new-born children suffering from brain damage or crippling disease and with persons living in coma and existing physically by mechanical means, no decision must be made without deep heart-searching. Such deaths must be made sacrificially, must be given as a 'making holy', as a blessing.

If I have strayed from the common notion of sacrifice, it is because here we are faced with many problems. We hear of soldiers who 'sacrificed their lives' or who 'were sacrificed' in war. Are these true sacrifices or not? In some instances soldiers did accept death, or at least the risk of death, willingly; in other instances this is not so. War is undoubtedly evil, but sometimes it is necessary to read the injuction to harm no-one as an injuction to judge between two possible harms. One should perhaps 'harm' the psychopathic killer, the racist, the terrorist, to preserve the lives of other people. Witches, in general, however, prefer to frustrate the wrongdoer rather than damage him, to influence his will, his decisions, and to give him the opportunity to turn his life in other directions.

The ritual sacrifice of living creatures other than humans presents fewer problems. The rhythm of the natural world is based upon a system of inter-relationships, and one of these is that between predator and prey, host and parasite. We feed upon one another. The human race is carnivorous; though particular human beings are able to discipline themselves into being vegetarians, the majority eat the flesh of animals, fish and birds, and some eat reptiles and insects. The killing of creatures for meat is not therefore a breach of natural law, nor is the breeding of animals for food. To sacrifice a bull or a chicken or a sheep is therefore permissible, provided that the desire is, indeed, to 'make holy'.

Here we come to the nub of the problem: the act of sacrifice. It must, first of all, be done humanely and without causing suffering. Secondly it must be done reverently. Thirdly it must be done as part of a feast in which all share, so that the meat and its blessings are part of the celebration. Unused portions which cannot be turned to good use should be burned in the fire.

In the past, occultists would 'sacrifice' an animal, often a black cockerel, largely in order to derive psychic energy from the positive explosion of released power that comes from sudden and violent death. This energy was then used by the magician to 'raise' spirits to be commanded, and to give the magician additional personal power. Witches do not seek power in this fashion. Their power comes not from the stimulation of the ego but from the subjection of the ego to the life-force of the universe. Witches do not make sacrifices of the kind I have described.

Witches do, however, 'make holy' many objects they use, and transform them in the process. The burning of a candle is a sacrificial act, a giving-up, a transforming. The burning of leaves, twigs, flowers, in a fire is a sacrifice. So is the burning of incense. When anything is consumed in the fire during a magical act or ritual, it is 'made holy' by being given up to the Goddess. Moreover, there is a 'making holy' in every blessing given at a meal, especially if a token portion of that meal is 'yielded up' by being consumed in the fire or buried in the earth.

There are some Wiccan sacrificial rituals, but they take the form of returning, symbolically, to the Goddess, to the life-force, some of her gifts. Thus one may make a sacrifice to the Goddess as Sea-Mother by floating something out upon the tide or throwing it in the water, as some of the Canadian west coast Indians return the first catch of the season to the river or sea. One may sacrifice to the Corn Goddess in the traditional rite of burning the first sheaf of corn that is reaped. One may sacrifice to the Earth Goddess by burying something appropriate, and to the Sky Goddess by sending smoke from a fire up into the sky. The Goddess of the Woodland may be worshipped by hanging gifts upon trees. Sacrifices of this kind will be found in all nature-orientated cultures. In the far past some of these sacrifices were bloody and brutal; they are not so today.

Witches do make sacrifices but not blood sacrifices, and before contemplating any sacrifice they ask themselves, 'Is this part of the natural rhythm of the universe?' 'Does this bring harm to anyone?' and 'Is this a making holy?'

14 Do witches stick pins in dolls?

Some witches use actual images of the people they wish to heal, bless or influence, but in these days it is usual to make use of photographs as aids to visualization of the subject. Some witches also use dolls to help them visualize the actual body of a person more vividly.

In the past these dolls were called 'poppets', and it was said by the persecutors of witches that they were used solely for cursing, either by sticking pins in the dolls or by mutilating them in some other way. The assumption was made that sticking pins into poppets was invariably intended to be destructive. A moment's thought, however, tells one that touching, or probing, a source of pain can well be healing. Witches may indeed have been early practitioners of acupuncture; they were certainly aware of acupressure and of the importance of using touch. Be that as it may, witches today certainly do study acupressure and the various kinds of massage. They do not use acupuncture unless they are professionally trained to do so by recognized institutions and are already members of the medical profession. In the main they tend to use therapeutic touch, as do the over 15,000 nurses who have studied the technique with Dr. Krieger at New York University and elsewhere. Therapeutic touch can be used to some extent at a distance from the sufferer by means of strong visualization, and dolls may be used in this procedure.

15 Are witches drunken?

Witches are no more addicted to alcohol than other people, but most of their celebrations and feasts do involve drinking.

There is a reason for this. Some have suggested that witchcraft rites are descended from the inebriated orgies of the Bacchanalia, and the feasts of the followers of Dionysus, in which intoxication resulted in wild songs and dances. This may or may not be so, but it is certain that alcohol is a depressant that lessens the efficiency of that side of the brain which deals with rational thought, logical reasoning and matters of nice consideration and speculation.

Thus the other side of the brain, which is more concerned with the emotional and the intuitive, is given more power. The consequence of this is, as we have all observed, that the drunken person (if not too drunk to function) speaks emotionally, expresses suppressed feelings, operates by instinct and intuition rather than reason, and feels a sense of great release. Therefore, if one is attempting to build up an energy that must operate non-rationally and intuitively, it is quite sensible to assist oneself with an alcoholic drink.

I am not, of course, suggesting that magic is performed in a drunken state. I am merely pointing out that a carefully chosen amount of wine or beer or spirits can be used as an aid and that this has always been a technique used by members of the Craft. Indeed, one of the reasons why puritans have objected, and still object, to strong drink may be their realization that drink can open gateways they would rather leave closed.

Witches have also, in the past, used hallucinogenic mushrooms for the same purpose, as Robert Graves and others have pointed out. The object has never been self-indulgence, however, but always the acquisition, simultaneously, of energy and perception.

All this may sound as if a teetotaller who does not use drugs cannot be a witch. That would be absurd. There are other ways to achieve the desired result, and no one is going to be debarred from a coven because he or she drinks only water and prefers bread and butter to magic mushrooms.

16   Do witches have sexual orgies?

The short answer is 'No.' This must, however, be qualified.

Wicca began as a fertility religion, and its rituals were often intended to increase the fertility of women as well as of the natural world. Some of these rituals involved sexual acts between members of the coven and/or between the male leader of a coven and the women members. For this latter, for obvious practical reasons, an artificial phallus was used. Acts of this kind were serious acts of magical worship, not mere lechery. To the witch the act of sexual union between woman and man is the bringing-together of the two complementary parts of the universe in a 'marriage' which results in an ecstatic union of flesh and spirit. This attitude is present in many other cultures: one thinks immediately of the Yin and Yang of China, the tantric practices of India and Tibet, the customs of the early Polynesians and Micronesians and many others. The miracle of Christ in transforming water to wine at the marriage in Cana was not the act of a divinely gifted bar-tender: it was an expression of the spiritual transformation which takes places at the moment of complete sexual union. The commonplace is transfigured for both the participants and those who share in the celebration.

Witches regard the act of sex as an act of love— love not only of the chosen partner but of the Goddess/God unity which is the life and soul of this world. Physical love is not a sin but a reverence, not a guilt but a joy.

Some present-day covens make use of sexual rituals. The ritual coupling of priest and priestess, or of members of the coven, is, however, usually performed privately and at the close of group rituals. Moreover the partners are usually those who already have an established sexual relationship. Casual promiscuity is as rare among witches as among members of Christian congregations.

Nevertheless, it must be pointed out that witches differ from the majority of Christian sects and from Mohammedans and others in seeing nothing shameful in the exposure of the human body and in regarding group nudity as healthy and natural. Moreover, witches are not obsessed with sexuality, as are many people who, quite understandably, find forbidden fruit exceedingly attractive, for to them the fruit is not forbidden. This may be because the kind of immense energy, the delight in energy and its use and release, the sense of transcending the limits of personality, the sense of unity with the life-force, which most people find only in sex, is found by witches in their rituals, in their summoning-up and use of psychic energy and in their private acts of magic and worship. This is, of course, also true of people who devote themselves wholly to other religions, of the Sufis and Dervishes in their mystical dances, of many celibate Christian priests and others. The difference is perhaps that the witches do not exclude sexual desire from their religion; they include it and make it a part of the whole.

17 Do witches indulge in wild dances?

In the past, dances formed an important part of many meetings and sabbats. Some of these dances became known as folk-dances and are nowadays performed by groups which study this art form and present it on stage in ballet and opera. Famous dances such as the maypole dance and the Floral Dance of Cornwall are still performed in the open air, and the whole community may take part.

Witches of today do not use dance as frequently as one might think. The reason may lie partly in the difficulty, in past times, of conducting a full-blown dance with appropriate music in secret. Centuries of persecution took their toll of many rituals and celebrations which originally involved the whole village community. Nevertheless, dance does still play a part in witchcraft. Music and dance release the dancer in part from the bondage of restrictive reason; the body moves rhythmically and instinctively; the dancer, by the very act of dancing, expresses universal harmony. Moreover, when one dances barefooted in the open air, one is in direct physical contact with the earth and the earth's energy field, and sharing this experience with other dancers, whether one is linked with them physically or not. For witches, as for Sufis and Dervishes, dance is a way of calling up energy and feeling at one with the rhythmic life of the universe.

The witch's dance may be divided into several categories. The first takes the form of sympathetic magic and may be called the mime dance, imitating, in its symbolic movements, what the group wishes to happen. A clear example is the rain dance that is to be found in many cultures. Another is the mating dance in which couples advance, retreat, chase and capture. These folk-dances became sophisticated as time went by and can be seen in the patterns of many square-dances as well as such elegant ballroom dances as the minuet and such romps as the Paul Jones. Modern ballroom dancing, especially the waltz and the tango, clearly derive from mating dances.

One form of the mime dance relates to myths and legends and to the seasons of the year. There are dances which mime and celebrate the gathering of fruit, the reaping of corn, the rebirth of the God or the Goddess, at the appropriate season, and so forth. Some of these dances can be seen in the work of the morris dancers whose performances derive clearly from ancient folk-magic.

A second category is the ring dance, in which the dancers move in a circle, usually around a bonfire. The rhythm of this dance is simple, though there are various ways of interpreting it. One may dance 'heel and toe', to quote an old witch song, skip, twirl in between steps, hold hands with one's neighbours or look first to one side then to another, making one's head, as it were, join the dance. This particular dance is one to create energy and unity and is one way of expressing the turning of the wheel of the year.

The ring dance, because of its miming and rhythm of the year, can also be placed in the third category, which I will call the cosmic dance, in which the dancers mimic not only the changes of the seasons but also the rhythm of the universe itself. The most important dance of this kind is the spiral dance, in which the dancers, moving in a circle, spiral inwards to the centre and then out again. This has many significances. Firstly it mimes the spiritual journey from the outer to the inward reality and then the necessary return to the world of action from the world of contemplation. It images death and rebirth. It images the waning and the waxing of the moon. It is, indeed, the expression, in dance, of the cyclic nature of the universe and of life in the universe.

This movement to the centre and then out to the periphery of a circle has been important to a number of cultures. We see it expressed in the design of mazes, where one must perform the same kind of journey. It is probable that originally all mazes were circular, but in time their religious significance was lost and they became simply games and diversions for visitors to the estates of the rich; later they became board-games and puzzles for children. The spiral can also be found in designs on mosaics and on textiles in many cultures, and delineated inside the domes of many temples. One might even argue that the domes and cupolas on religious buildings in countries around the world are related to spiral symbolism.

18   Do witches cast spells?

Witches certainly cast spells, either alone or in the coven. Some spells are organized verbally, the word carrying the whole of the intent. Some involve the use of talismans that the witch must give to the person to be affected. Some use neither words nor specific objects but are simply made by a kind of projection of the imagination.

Spells work in many ways. The majority can be described as analogous to radio messages: a 'transmission' is sent out to the inner 'deep mind' of someone, and this message reinforces that person's desire to recover health or changes that person's intentions and attitudes. The majority of witches concentrate upon spells that heal or protect or bring good fortune. It is sometimes necessary, however, to work a spell to bind someone to a particular course of action or prevent their doing something wrong. These spells which curtail activity or even act as a curse are usually discussed carefully by the whole coven before they are transmitted. Sometimes a curse is sent upon people who harm others, in order to prevent their continuing to do harm.

The power used in spells has been variously labelled. Some have referred to it in terms of telepathic force; some have seen it as being a kind of electro-magnetism; others have called it 'the Odic Force'. However it is labelled, the force remains as a powerful means of change and alteration and one that, in witches' belief, must not be used lightly, for whatever 'message' is transmitted returns at least threefold upon the sender. Consequently, those witches who work curses (however justified), or who seek to bind others to their will must take particular care to protect themselves by other kinds of magic and to assure themselves that what they are doing is in full accord with the ethics of the Craft.

19 How ancient are witches' spells?

Spells, to be effective, must be newly made or re-made by each spell-caster so that they carry personal intent. The formulae on which new spells are made may, however, be very old indeed. Many spells of today are similar in structure to those found in the Atharva Veda which was composed thousands of years ago. Others remind one of spells found in pre-Christian cultures of the Middle East and Egypt. The Gaelic *carmina Gadelica* are certainly of considerable antiquity and, though Christianized in part, clearly came from pre-Christian Celts.

There is no particular virtue in a spell's age. It is simply that spells which have been handed down over the centuries must have been considered efficient and are therefore worth studying, but ancient spells cannot cope with all the complexities of modern life, and so entirely new spells are being created. Moreover, our twentieth-century understanding of the human body, for example, is greater than that of earlier centuries, and therefore our healing spells can be more precise than was possible hundreds of years ago.

20 Do witches make magic potions?

From time immemorial witches have been herbalists and have made medicine for their community. They have also been the guardians of much other traditional lore. Their reputation as herbalists led to their being accused, from time to time, of being poisoners. Indeed, the word 'poisoner' is mistranslated as 'witch' in the well-known biblical command 'Thou shalt not suffer a witch to live.' When a medicine is ineffective and the patient dies, the doctor may nowadays be sued for malpractice; in earlier times the 'wise woman' would be accused of being a poisoner and a witch. Many witches today are expert and learned herbalists, but they would not call their cough syrups, spring tonics and skin salves magical. They are no more magical than aspirin. In the past, however, these medicaments were regarded as magical because their operation was mysterious to the general populace.

Some books on witchcraft do include potions which are clearly not the product of scientific understanding but are symbolic. The recipient's belief in the potion may well lead to the right results, as may the witch's conviction that it will work, and the amount of Odic Force (p.23) he or she puts into its preparation. Nevertheless many so-called magical potions given in books that popularize the notion of the witch are extremely silly, and some are likely to cause little more than indigestion.

Witches are, however, concerned to alter and affect people's attitudes and states of mind. They therefore make use of aromatic herbs, oils and incense and develop recipes that will change people's moods and affect them emotionally. They are, one might say, perfumiers as well as herbalists.

In making up medicaments or perfumes or bath oils, however, more goes into the manufacture than practical skill. Witches bless their products as they make them; they concoct their potions at a time that the moon is in the right phase or when the astrological situation is propitious. There is no aspect of the craft that does not make use of the Odic Force and take into account the powers of the natural and spiritual world.

21 Do witches make magic charms?

The answer is 'Yes.' Witches may either actually create charms, making them from metal or other materials if they have the necessary skills, or they may imbue an already existing object with the power to send messages, to transmit their intent. Most charms are protective, and many are worn around the neck as a pendant, as some Christians wear a cross or a St Christopher's medal. Some are placed beneath the pillow to help give calm sleep or to cure insomnia. Some are buried under the threshold of the house to guard the inhabitants from harm.

Charms are used because they continually transmit their messages, whereas a spoken spell does not necessarily continue working at full strength after a time. Moreover, the person who has the charm, or talisman, is reminded of its intent every time he or she sees or feels it. Some talismans are traditional, such as the rabbit's or hare's foot; some are made of written words on parchment or paper; some are elaborately made in the occult tradition and involve the use of precious stones. Most witches prefer simple charms which they empower themselves. Store-bought talismans have no power; the power must be given them.

22   Do witches ride broomsticks?

The popular image of a hag flying through the air astride a broomstick derives from not one but from several practices of the craft.

Firstly, in the past, all households owned a broom for purely practical purposes. Witches would, indeed, disguise the wand or staff they used for magical purposes by binding twigs around the end, to hide the carving on it which might betray its magical function.

Secondly, at certain times of the year country folk would perform a dance around the cornfield in order to increase the rate of growth, mimicking the rising of the corn by leaping into the air. This is not as absurd as it may seem. We have now discovered that plants respond to human emotion, that cows give more milk when played music and that all kinds of plants flourish when they are talked to. The witches' leaping dance, astride a pole which simulated the straightness and strength of the corn, therefore makes a good deal of sense. This dance would normally be performed by the light of the full moon, which affects the world of nature as it also affects man (the word 'lunatic', derived from the Latin *luna*, the moon, stems from the observation that the full moon has a disturbing effect on the psyche). Thus anyone observing the leaping broomstick dance of witches at the full moon could be expected to think of flying.

This broomstick dance became confused with other accounts of witches flying through the night to take part in meetings and orgies. A number of witches have testified to this night-flying, which was achieved by rubbing a magical ointment on the body. It is now clear that the ointment was hallucinogenic and caused fantasies not dissimilar to those caused by LSD and other fashionable drugs of our century, and that the hallucinations were shaped by the witches' own minds. There is evidence of witches swearing that they have flown, when they have been under observation the whole time, apparently asleep, but sometimes clearly experiencing orgasm.

Many recipes have been suggested for this ointment, which is rubbed on the pulse of the wrists and elsewhere. Some of the materials suggested are aconite, belladonna, cinquefoil, parsley, watercress, henbane, oil and, absurdly, the fat of boiled babies and human flesh; bats' blood is also mentioned. The trouble is that none of these mixtures, however organized, can get into the bloodstream through unbroken skin. It has been suggested that in the past witches were so flea-bitten that the drug could penetrate through these open wounds. It seems unlikely.

One recipe, when the element of the grotesque is removed, makes sense. This calls for a mixture of babies' fat (for which one must read pork fat, mutton fat, goose-grease, lard of any kind), black millet and boiled toad. Black millet is a fungus found on millet and is ergot, which is a hallucinogenic. Witches kept toads as pets, and when toads are excited or frightened, they exude a milky substance called toads' milk, a substance which was, we know, once used by witches. From toads' milk (and from toadstools) scientists have extracted a drug called Bufotenine, an alkaloid which, though insoluble in water, is soluble in alcohol and in dilute acids and alkalis. (The ordinary household is rarely short of weak acid as a solvent if it is needed. Urine would do. So would vinegar.) It has the property of penetrating the skin and going straight into the bloodstream, producing the same hallucinogenic effects as LSD but with brighter colour effects. It works rapidly, producing its effects in fifteen to thirty minutes, and these last for between one and two hours. It produces not only hallucinations but contractions of the intestinal and uterine muscles, so it seems clear that it could easily induce orgasm and that the orgasm itself would induce sexual fantasies.

Existing accounts of night-flying by witches make it clear that the latent period between the application of the ointment and the beginning of the hallucination is not long (as it is with many hallucinogenics), and the flight does not last more than an hour or so. It seems clear therefore that Bufotenine, in its original form as toads' milk, is the missing element in all the recipes that have so far been handed down, and that boiled toad is simply a disguised reference to this.

Contemporary witches do not use flying-ointment. If they wish to use hallucinogenics, they use those made in laboratories. Most witches, however, are not drug-users. They are able to have visions without that kind of stimulus.

23 Do witches still use broomsticks?

A good many witches possess brooms of the old pattern, partly for symbolic reasons and partly because a broom is useful. One cannot use a vacuum cleaner symbolically to sweep anything away, and the magical sweeping-away of unwanted sickness, disorder or even unhappiness can be important to a household. An old rhyme quoted by Doreen Valiente runs, 'If you sweep the house with blossomed broom in May, you will sweep the head of the house away', which testifies to the symbol's potency. The broom has been a phallic symbol in the past; indeed, a broom is sometimes tied to the top of the maypole on May Day.

Brooms may be made of many kinds of twig, not only those of broom itself. One old formula is a staff of ash, twigs of birch for the brush, and the binding strips of willow. Another combines a hazel staff with oak twigs bound together with birch strips. However, not all witches can achieve these formulae, and nowadays the important thing is the broom itself.

24 Do witches foretell the future and are they psychic?

No one can systematically foretell the future. There have been many well-documented instances of precognition, but they seem to have happened at random. Many witches can, however, by making use of numerology, the tarot deck of cards or other techniques, perceive the pattern a person's life is making and can therefore deduce what pattern it is likely to make in the future unless deliberate and considerable changes are made. Sometimes a witch (or anyone else for that matter) can as a result of deep meditation and intuitive probing, have a sudden burst of illumination. Sometimes a person's aura will be seen so vividly and clearly by the witch that it's shape and colour will reveal where that person is heading. Because witches are practised in using their intuitions and because they know how to make use of various traditional techniques, they tend to be better at perceiving what is likely to occur in the future than are other people. Among the techniques used are those of palmistry, geomancy, casting the runes and crystal-gazing, or scrying. Many witches also make use of the Chinese system of the I Ching.

All witches are more than usually sensitive to the 'vibrations' of places and people, and they become more sensitive as they continue to pursue their craft. They are not, however, necessarily 'psychics', mediums or clairvoyants, though they may be. After all, any religion may include psychics among its members.

Having said this, I must add that it is incumbent upon every witch to develop psychic sensitivity to the best of his or her ability, and that all witches do learn to read the tarot or the runes and practise psychometry, though some witches are more expert than others.

25   How do witches regard death?

Death is not an ending but a beginning. It is a gateway. When we die, we move out of this time-space continuum into another dimension of which we know almost nothing. Witches believe in neither Heaven nor Hell, and for them the concept of entering upon eternity is meaningless. We are all in eternity. We are all caught up in a never-ending life-process. This process may lead us, after one death, to return to this time-space continuum for another life. This new life will be partly conditioned by the previous one, for, according to the doctrine of karma, the lessons we have failed to learn in one life we may carry partially into its successor.

Normally we have no recollection of past lives, but they can be recalled in a ritual of regression. In this ritual the witch, by means of light hypnotism, sends the mind of the subject through the birth-barrier back into time, and the subject recalls past lives. Sometimes these past lives are so clearly envisioned that they can be checked out by searching historical records; most times they are not. In some instances it seems likely that the subject does not so much recall as imagine a past life, but, as William Blake pointed out, 'Anything possible to be imagined is an image of the Truth', and the imagination or fantasy of the subject simply provides invented details for the essence of past experience or projects subconscious self-knowledge back upon a scene of time past.

Witches do not therefore grieve for the dead. Like everyone else, they grieve for their own loss of friends and family, but this grief is soon overcome by the feeling of gladness at the new opportunities the dead one is being given.

26   Do witches perform ceremonies in graveyards?

There are two kinds of burial-grounds. One is simply a field in which corpses are buried, the graves being marked by memorial stones. The second is a place with a strong energy field which has been used as a pagan meeting-place and has come to be used as a graveyard. These, in Europe, are mostly the lands around a church, or churchyards. Witches have never made use of burial-grounds as such, but only of 'holy' places, which might or might not have been used for burials. These days witches do not meet in churchyards, even those which were once pagan gathering-places, as they have no desire to offend members of other religions.

Graveyards are not, as many believe, haunted by the spirits of the dead. The dead leave no imprint where their bodies are buried, though they may leave an imprint where they have suffered or died. The only strong emotions left as imprints in graveyards are those of the mourners.

27   Do witches perform exorcisms?

Some witches do 'lay ghosts'. The form of exorcism they use is much gentler than that used by some Christian churches with 'bell, book and candle'. The ghost is regarded as being a misplaced spirit that has failed to make the transition from this life to the next: Or it may be simply an imprint of strong emotions left in a particular place, causing that place to become disturbed, to suffer from strange noises, patches of cold, doors opening and shutting of their own accord. Sometimes the ghost is simply a feeling, an atmosphere that depresses. The witch's task is firmly and politely to send away the misplaced spirit or to bless and heal the house wounded by past emotions. All exorcisms leave a kind of emptiness which must be filled by a blessing. Indeed, most witches take great care to bless any house or apartment into which they or their friends move. There are always some traces of past occupants and of the emotional lives of others, and these can be disturbing. Some witches are expert ghost-hunters and exorcists.

28 Why is midnight considered 'the witching hour'?

There are several reasons. The first is that midnight is the middle of the witches' day, for that day stretches from noon to noon. It begins in light and it ends in light. This is why all sabbats are celebrated on the eve of the day marked in the calendar.

The second reason is that, when all the business of the normally calculated day is over, there is more peace in which to work and contemplate. There are no intrusions from the tensions of the worka-day world.

The third reason is that the moon is regarded as a presence of the Goddess, and therefore night-time is appropriate for any celebration of her.

Finally, in days past, it was unwise to celebrate in the full light of day for fear of discovery, and so it has become traditional for all witchcraft proceedings to take place at least after dark, though not necessarily at midnight. Because the number nine is a cube of three and the Goddess is threefold, nine o'clock is often chosen.

29 Why do witches do their magic in a circle?

There are several reasons for the use of the circle. First, the circle symbolizes unity, wholeness and the circular movement of the seasons and of what has been called 'the wheel of stars'. It is also an extremely ancient symbol of community, for if one gathers people in a circle, no one person can be at the head of it: all are equal who stand, sit or kneel round its periphery. Witchcraft is, or should be, democratic. All are equal, certainly as regards social standing. One of the reasons adduced for witches working either naked ('sky-clad') or in identical black cloaks is that this prevents social distinctions being made.

If the gathering is in the form of a rectangle, one person, or a small group of persons at one end of the rectangle, may dominate the rest. If, as in most Christian churches, the gathering is in the form of a rectangular block of worshippers with prominent people facing this block, one has a hierarchical situation. Moreover, in a group where it is essential for each member to be able to see the other members, to share their feelings as expressed in their faces or by body language, and to join with them in the creation and use of collective energies, the circle is the only practical arrangement. In a circle one can even see the expression of one's immediate neighbour, which does not happen if the formation is a square.

Moreover, if one dances, or even walks, around in a circle, one is imitating the movement of the wheel of life and the cyclic nature of the universe.

Long tradition tells us that the circle should be nine feet in diameter. This is, of course, absurd if there are only a few people in the gathering. Nine feet is, however, about right for the maximum number of Craft members permitted a coven in conventional thinking. It will hold thirteen people, unless, of course, they are all somewhat stout. Nine is a magical number, and so it is tempting to permit tradition to become dogma and make the nine-foot requirement a 'law', and some groups do take this attitude.

The centre of the circle is usually given prominence by either an altar or a bonfire. One must have something to circle around, after all. The movement is usually clockwise, or sunwise, which is called 'deosil', this being a positive movement, a sharing of the movement of the universe. Anticlockwise movement is referred to as 'widdershins' or 'tuathal'; in most traditions this movement is used when the intent of the circle is to 'unwind' or negate something.

There are several different ways of laying out the circle. The central altar or table usually bears symbols representing the four elements— earth, air, fire and water. Some witches also place lights or candles at the four points of the compass. Some make the central altar elaborate; some prefer simplicity. Witches who lean towards the occult tradition tend to dress their altars beautifully and to insist that the circle be drawn by a consecrated sword; others are content to draw the circle with a piece of chalk or even with a stick. In this, as in all matters of witchcraft, it is the intent, informed by imagination, which counts.

The circle will be drawn around the group by the group's leader;

he or she may be the invariable leader of the group, or the leader for that particular occasion. The leader, having drawn the circle around the group three times, will close the 'door' behind. Now all are in the circle, and the business of raising the cone of power can begin.

30   What is a cone of power?

When the coven is assembled within the circle, the leader will invoke the Goddess, which means simply to ask her presence and her power. Then the leader will guide the members in calling up energy until all are ready. This may be done in several ways. One is for the leader to ask all to feel energy rising up from the centre of the earth, through the legs, the torso, to the shoulders and the arms and then the hands, and to ask all the group to envisage their arms and hands as interlacing with those of their neighbours. The actual holding of hands is not necessary, though it may be done. Then the leader directs all to concentrate upon the work to be done, to join in one vision, and this creates a 'cone' of energy. Some sensitive people have seen this cone, as they see auras, and have maintained that it rises from the circle as a silver-blue light. The group then concentrates on 'beaming' this energy in the direction and with the intent that has been decided. The process takes little time. No one can keep up that pitch of concentration for very long. When all feel that the message has been sent, the cone is allowed to subside, and the leader will say a few further words to the Goddess and then open the 'door', and all will leave the circle (moving deosil) by that opening. All must then 'ground' the energy that is left over. This can be done by kneeling and striking the earth (or the floor) a number of times or by dipping hands into water or rubbing them with salt.

Before this whole ritual begins, it is as well for the group to anoint their 'third eyes' (the pineal glands situated in the centre of the forehead just above eyebrow level) with a little blessed oil and ask for protection. Some of the energy released may otherwise 'bounce back' and cause undue nervous tension or even harm.

This description of the creation and use of the circle is more straightforward than many you will find in books of rituals, and I must add that some groups, while following the basic pattern I have given, do make the whole process more complex and more theatrical. In some traditions, the priest and priestess may occupy the centre of the circle and perform rituals at the altar. There are numerous variations, many of which owe more to the occult tradition than to the customs of the Craft, which usually deals simply and directly in all its ways.

31   Do witches use hypnosis?

Hypnosis has been a Wiccan skill for centuries. Indeed, an English law of the thirteenth century condemned 'Enchantment, as those who send people to sleep'. The witches used then, as now, a witch ball, which is a ball that reflects light, its surface often made up of a number of small pieces of mirror or polished metal. It is hung from a ceiling or dangled in front of the subject, in the way in which bright objects have been used since the beginning of the nineteenth century by doctors using hypnosis. Other methods of hypnosis, such as eye-to-eye contact and softly murmured words, are also used. Witches, in their healing practices, make considerable use of auto-suggestive techniques, as do doctors.

This hypnotic skill explains why witches have, in the past, been credited with turning people into animals. As we know from many stage performances, a hypnotist can make a person believe himself or herself to be a dog or a cat, and bark or mew accordingly. Post-hypnotic suggestion can also cause people to behave strangely. Those who use hypnosis irresponsibly, or to alarm and tease, are, of course, asking for trouble. Nevertheless, hypnotism can be a powerful force for good. If one can make a person believe strongly that healing is occurring, or has occurred, the belief will, in many cases, become reality, for the body is obedient to belief.

32   Do witches have familiars?

'Familiars' are, supposedly, household animals that contain or embody a spirit who advises the witch and does his or her bidding. The notion seems to have arisen from several sources. One is the belief by occultists of some sects that 'supernatural' forces can enter into animals and that the Devil may appear in the form of an animal or appear accompanied by one, quite frequently a black dog. Another source is the observation by people who do not own pets themselves that pet-owners speak to their pets and frequently receive what appears to be replies. A third source is the distrust many people feel for nocturnal animals, and in particular the cat and its ability to see in the dark.

Witches, being very much of the opinion that other creatures are part of a universal harmony rather than alien forms deserving of no respect, have tended to have a more amiable relationship with the natural world than have many of their contemporaries. They kept pets, and they talked to them and trained them to respond to orders. Their pets were part of the household economy. The dogs dealt with the rats and with marauders and helped with the hunting. The cats kept the mouse population down. Hares were kept as we keep rabbits, as companions and, eventually for food and fur. Toads may seem a stranger form of pet, but in a house or cottage with straw-covered floors, what better creature to deal with flies and fleas than a toad? Moreover 'toad's milk' is a hallucinogenic, and toads have the useful ability to suspend animation when placed in confinement without food or water for long periods: you do not have to send a toad to a kennel when you go away on a holiday. Both songbirds and those birds that can mimic human speech to various degrees, such as the jackdaw, magpie and raven, were also kept as pets.

After a time the relationship of the pet with its 'master' or 'mistress' becomes close, and nowadays most of us are amused and do not think it 'odd' when a cat is taken for walks on or without a lead, when a bird rides around on its owner's shoulder or when a parrot or mynah bird calls out 'Hello there!' when we enter the house. In earlier days, before Pavlov explained 'conditioning', this was regarded not merely as odd but as 'unnatural' or even 'supernatural'.

Most of the witches I know have pets to whom they talk and who obey at least some of the commands they are given. Most other people I know have pets also. This is, however, only part of the truth. Dogs, cats, birds and toads have perceptive abilities which are denied to most human beings. Dogs are quick to sense the presence of ghosts and of what we may call 'unfriendly vibrations' in people. They feel the approach of earthquakes and natural disasters long before men do so, for all their seismographic skills. They react strongly to the death of an absent member of the family long before that death is known to have occurred. This may not be true of all dogs, but it is true of a great many.

Cats are also psychically sensitive and appear to be able to see 'presences' which humans cannot. They are also ingenious and highly intelligent creatures. Toads have a similar reputation among those who have studied them in domestic surroundings. Toads and cats have, of course, been associated with spiritual power for many centuries, and the cat, which the Romans introduced into Britain from Egypt, was, under the name of Bast, regarded as one aspect of the Great Goddess, Isis.

Because of this, some household pets, particularly cats, are used by some witches to assist in divination or in making choices between possible lines of action. This is commonly done by laying out objects, each of which has a particular significance, and manoeuvring the animal into selecting one of them. Some witches use their 'familiars' almost as scrying-glasses, talking to them, caressing them and asking them questions, believing that the answer which comes to the witch is provided by the extra-sensory perception of the familiar.

33   *What implements do witches use?*

In 'the burning times', the years of persecution, witches used very simple tools, and ones that were common household objects. These were a knife, a knotted cord, a staff or wand (disguised as a broom), a three-legged cooking-pot, a drinking cup and tallow candles. A wooden staff was another usual posession. This frequently culminated in a 'V' shape to provide a grip for the thumb, but the two arms of the "v" were privately regarded as symbolizing the two horns of the god. Wherever it was not too dangerous, this staff or "stang" would be carved with symbols, and it might be crowned by a real set of horns. Witches also had a store of salt, pork fat (the common base for apothecaries' salves) and, of course, berries and herbs. Beeswax was also kept in the house and used for making talismans and poppets ; such objects could easily and quickly be melted down when danger threatened. Many witches kept bees to ensure a good supply of wax as well as honey which they used in their medicines.

When the laws against witchcraft were repealed and Wicca was no longer illegal, the tools became more elaborate. To the list above was added an incense-burner (early witches simply threw fragrant herbs on the fire). The knife was replaced by two knives, one black-handled (the Athame) and one white-handled. The cup became a chalice. On cup and on knives and incense-burner magical inscriptions would be painted or incised, these symbols often deriving from the occult rather than the witchcraft tradition. Some witches insist that the knives must be made by the witch himself or herself. A mirror was also added to the list of implements; though this appears to have been in use in early times, it was not a common household object of the poor. Witches did not use mirrors as scrying-glasses, but water in a black pot, or water into which a black stone had been placed.

The pentacle, or pentagram, a five-pointed star made up of two interpenetrating triangles and drawn in one unbroken line, is used by some witches, although it derives from the Hebraic tradition. It is, however, a powerful symbol that shows the five senses in unity, the fusion of masculine and feminine, and the four elements of life together with the spirit. It is a very ancient symbol indeed, and examples of it have been found in the ruins of Babylon. Witches often wear a pentagram as an identifying badge, as Christians wear a cross.

Most witches have a spell table or altar which is used only for ritual and magical work. This altar frequently has an image of the Goddess, but not always. Candles grace the altar. Candles are traditional implements, but the early simple tallow candles have been replaced by coloured wax candles and there are now many spells which use black, white, red, yellow or green candles for specific purposes.

Many witches have their own personal implements. These may take the form of pendants, rings, oddly shaped stones, intricately patterned spell boxes and so forth.

The implements are not absolutely necessary. They are simply a means to assist the mind to concentrate, to help to get into the right frame of mind and to help in the summoning and transmission of energy. An efficient witch can work without any implements at all, though it is difficult to work powerful magic without them.

Some witches feel that it shows proper reverence for the Goddess and God to have an elaborate altar furnished with silver candlesticks, thuribles and so forth, and to have an antique and valuable image of the Goddess. Others feel that this approach is not proper for a tradition in which material wealth means little and in which ostentation has never played a part; they feel that the occult tradition, with its emphasis upon elaborate rituals and the use of precious metals and jewels, may have caused this change, and they deplore it. The vast majority of witches like their altars to look beautiful and are happy to have lovely things but are not averse to working on the kitchen table with quite unimpressive tools if that is what is necessary, or even doing some magic without any tools at all when the situation demands it.

Nevertheless, so many questions have been asked about the witch's implements in the past that it may be as well to answer some of them in detail.

34   Why do witches have cauldrons?

The three-legged iron cooking-pot of olden days was central to the economy of the household. In it the food was cooked, the water was boiled. It was, one might say, 'the great provider'. In both Greek and Celtic myths there are magical cauldrons into which dead and dismembered corpses are thrown and from which they arise as living men. The process of transforming inedible to edible food has been seen as changing death to life. Moreover, the cauldron, because of its full-bellied shape, is an image of womanhood and fertility. Its three legs remind one of the Triple Goddess.

Today, apart from its power as a symbol, the cauldron has other practical uses. It can be used not only for cooking for feasts, but also as a receptacle for the fires of the sabbats. Outdoor fires are dangerous in the hot, dry weather of summer, and often illegal. A fire held in a cauldron is safe. Moreover, it is traditional for the charred remains of the fire of one sabbat to be used in creating the fire for the next one. A charred piece of wood is usually wrapped up and kept for this purpose. It is, however, easier to keep the remains of the fire in the cauldron till the next time. The cauldron can also be used to hold material which should be burned, such as remnants of thread from binding spells, or gobs of wax fallen from candles.

35   What are the witch's cord and garter?

The witch's cord is called a girdle or cingulum, which is the Latin word for a girdle or a sword belt. Originally it was almost certainly a length of twine with knots in it for measuring. Nowadays it is a red cord or ribbon made of three six-foot lengths plaited together. Some witches tie knots in it so that it can be used to measure the radius of the magic circle and of both inner and outer circles with radii of four feet, four feet six inches and five feet six. Other witches do not use the cord for this purpose but simply as a belt. Red being the colour of vitality, it is a constant reminder of the life-force.

In the Middle Ages a garter was not like those of today. It was a long string or cord that was wound round the leg several times and was, therefore, very like the present-day witch's girdle. Like the girdle, it is a reminder of life's vitality and of the wearer's allegiance to the Old Religion. Present-day witches use modern garters of various kinds and colours. Some traditions adopt a green leather garter with silver buckles. Garters of snakeskin and of velvet have also been reported. The buckles or badges on the garter are usually of silver and of symbolic design. In some traditions the buckles indicate the rank of the wearer within the coven.

36   What is the witch's knife?

There are two knives used by witches, one with a black handle, which is called the Athame, and one white-handled knife. The Athame is generally regarded as the traditional implement, and some witches use it to draw the magic circle or other designs. Others do not use the knife to make the circle but use a staff or wand or, if indoors, chalk, or simply pace it out, moving round three times clockwise, (deosil).

The knife should be consecrated, as should all the implements used in magic. Some witches have quite elaborate forms of consecration, and some simply concentrate upon the implement and speak to it, giving it direction, one might say. Witches who are craftspeople may make their own knives; most witches pick up a knife that they feel drawn to in a junk shop. As these have been used for non-magical purposes, they have to be cleansed either by burying them in the earth for three days or by covering them with salt to remove whatever energies they have gathered before dedicating them to the service of the Goddess.

37   What is a scrying-glass?

The most usual kind of scrying-glass is a crystal ball, and scrying, in many instances, means crystal-gazing.

Not all scrying-glasses are of this kind, however. Some are concave mirrors, some are green or blue glass fisherman's floats, and some are black bowls containing water, thus becoming mirrors. Indeed, many reflecting surfaces have been used for scrying, including bowls of oil or even wine.

Scrying is the act of perceiving past the usual obstacles of time and space. It is not necessarily perceiving the future: it may simply bring to mind a person or event in another place. There are a number of different methods. One is to stare into the chosen implement or medium, letting one's mind go blank and allowing images to form as they do in that half-waking state before sleep when faces, people, places come unbidden to the mind. The process may be helped if the room is dark but for a single candle flame which may also be reflected in the mirror, pool or crystal ball. The scrier attempts to achieve a state of mild trance by a kind of self-hypnosis.

If a mirror or crystal ball is used or, as is sometimes the case, a polished black stone in a bowl of water, these implements should be wrapped up in black cloth (preferably silk) when they are not in use. This helps them retain the energy field they have been given during the scrying, and also ensures that when they are unwrapped they are immediately associated with scrying, and therefore work more quickly.

By no means all witches use scrying-glasses, for it is a skill that can be completely mastered only by those who are clairvoyant or extremely sensitive psychically. Nevertheless, with practice, most people can 'scry' a little.

38   What is a witch's mirror?

Some witches make use of mirrors for scrying, and these are usually of black glass, or glass whose reverse has been coated with black. Others use mirrors in casting spells, and these mirrors are usually silver-framed and backed. Mirrors intensify the light of candles and reflect it so that it seems to be shining in another dimension, and this therefore reinforces the spellcaster's sense of power. Because the space 'in' the mirror is not 'real' space but appears to give life another dimension, it also adds to the sense that spells can pass through the boundaries set upon us by time and space. It is, in short, a reinforcing device. The notion of the magic mirror has been used by a great many writers, from the author of *Snow White and the Seven Dwarfs* to Alfred, Lord Tennyson, in his poem 'The Lady of Shallott', and is featured nowadays in the comic strip 'The Wizard of Id'.

39   What is the witch's chalice?

The witch's chalice is a cup or goblet used in rituals and at meetings of the coven. It is usually made of silver or silver plate. It does not have a handle as, in drinking ritually, it is common to hold the chalice in both hands. It often bears a pattern the witch considers appropriate: some are specially engraved with text or names, and these may be written out in one of the magical alphabets.

The chalice in the rituals of some traditions is also used as a symbol of femininity, the yoni, and the union of man and woman, of Goddess and God, is symbolized by dipping a ritual sword into the cup. Red wine is drunk at a number of rituals and celebrations.

40   *Do witches have a secret alphabet for magical use?*

There is no real witch's alphabet. The witches of the past were usually illiterate. Reading and writing were taught by clerics only to other clerics and members of powerful families. Witches did, however, have a system of signs which they would use to give messages to other witches, just as Romanies chalk signs upon the gateposts of houses they have visited to tell other Romanies whether or not a visit would be worthwhile.

More elaborate alphabets were created by occultists, and there are many of these, the most popular being the Theban Alphabet. Others are the Alphabet of the Magi, the Celestial Alphabet, the Malachim Alphabet and an alphabet called '*Du Passage du Fleuve*', 'Passing the River'. Some witches use such alphabets to inscribe their working tools with words of dedication or power; this is, however, an occultist rather than a Craft tradition. Some witches use the ancient symbolic languages of runes, and some create their own system of signs.

41   *What are spell boxes?*

Spell boxes are common to many cultures and are not necessarily boxes at all. They are places where a written spell is hidden and left untouched, until the spell has completed its task. This is almost an instinct with children, especially in the country. Few country-born children can have failed to put 'secrets' in hollow trees, in holes in walls, under rocks. There is an old superstition that, if a person's name is written on a piece of paper and locked up in an otherwise empty drawer, that person will die. I have considerable doubts about this and believe that the superstition may be simply a melodramatic exaggeration of the spell-box method.

Most spell boxes are of wood, but they can be made of any material. Organic material is preferable. Some boxes are beautiful and elaborately carved: the country people of Thailand carve wooden spell boxes in the shapes of frogs, cats, rabbits and ducks, and these are charming in all senses of the word. Other boxes carry 'magical' designs upon them. Some Kashmiri boxes, not originally intended for magical purposes, are in the shape of hearts and are decorated with flowers. Boxes from India often have elaborate inlaid patterns, and Chinese boxes are delightfully lacquered or carved.

Spell boxes are also used for storing magical objects, especially talismans. The colour and shape of the box must be appropriate to the talisman it holds. One does not put a spell bringing peace of mind in a vivid orange box, for example; it should go in a pale blue box or a green one. The shape and colour must not conflict with the contents.

42   Why are the pentagram and hexagram important to witches?

The pentagram, or pentacle, and the hexagram, or Star of David, were not originally a part of the tradition of the Craft, but became part of it, possibly by way of occultism or possibly simply because these two symbols represent so clearly a part of the witches perception of the universe.

Let us take the hexagram first. It is composed of two triangles which interpenetrate each other, thus:

Triangles can be seen as plane representations of spirals or cones. Once this is noted, it becomes obvious that here we have a representation of the spiral dance. We also, however, have a representation of the theory of gyres propounded by W.B. Yeats, who saw all history as moving out from a central point in a spiral and then, as the outer rim of the spiral was reached, collapsing into another central point and beginning the process again. We can relate it also to the diagram we have been given of the DNA molecule, the double helix, the very source of life itself. It is also an excellent representation of the earth's magnetic field, which is in the form of a spiral and which, we are told, reverses its polarity after an uncountable number of centuries have passed.

There is an even odder fact to add to these. The electromagnetic fields of various menhirs (standing stones) in Wales have been proved to take the form of a spiral, and it has been shown that these spiral fields also reverse themselves. Thus the hexagram, the so-called Seal of Solomon, is an expression of an essential element in the nature of life and the universe.

When we turn to the pentacle, we can see the spirals again, but they are not quite in the same relationship as in the hexagram. The pentacle is composed of one unbroken line and, indeed, in drawing one, one is required to do so without lifting one's pencil from the paper. It is still composed of two interpenetrating spirals, however, as thus:

Here, moving from one point to another, we find that we can never reach a situation where the spiral collapses inwards, for we always arrive at the apex of another triangle or spiral. Moreover, as we move around the figure, we find we are moving in a circle. Indeed, many pentacles are enclosed within a circle to reinforce this symbolism.

The pentacle can be regarded as representing the five senses of man and, when displayed with one point uppermost, as a schematized portrait of a man, with a head, two arms and two legs. Also the five small triangles (the five senses) enclose a five-sided figure which can be regarded as the spiritual force which unifies the senses into a whole, and as an expression of the God/Goddess within us. Other interpretations abound. The five points are seen by some as the four elements of life controlled by spirit, this being the uppermost point. controlled by spirit, this being the uppermost point. One view is that the points, reading clockwise from the top should be taken as indicating ether, or the element of the spiritual at the summit, and then water, fire, earth and air in that order. To some witches the pentagram with two points pointing upwards suggests spirit controlled by matter. Madame Blavatsky, the founder of Theosophy, thought the reversed pentagram the symbol of the age of violence and darkness in which we live. Nevertheless a number of witches find the reversed pentagram positive and see the two upward points as the horns of the Goddess' consort, the horned god. The majority of witches, however, wear the pentagram with the single point upwards.

It is regarded not only as a symbol for meditation but also as a protective talisman, much as Christians regard the cross.

The pentagram not only has multiple symbolic reference to the relationship between matter and spirit but also represents the creative movement of the universe and the central rhythm of all life. It can also be seen as an image of the Goddess standing with her arms spread, and with the beginnings of new life in her belly.

43   How do witches dress?

There is no general agreement on this, as is the case with so much that has to do with witchcraft. Some witches work naked, or 'sky-clad', because they feel that clothing hampers the Odic Force or electromagnetic waves they intend to employ. The nakedness is partly qualified. Female witches usually wear a necklace of material they feel appropriate, and sometimes a silver bracelet (silver is sacred to Diana; it is Diana's metal). Male witches may also wear a pendant. Both may wear rings.

Other witches wear loose cowled robes, usually black, and are either barefoot or sandalled. The colour black is traditional, possibly because of its effectiveness as camouflage in the past, when night gatherings were interrupted by strangers, or possibly because black, in so many traditions, is the colour of wisdom. It also reminds one of night, when the moon rules the sky.

Various covens with special interests or tastes dress differently. Some female witches wear the black conical hat displayed in many witch caricatures. This, originally a common form of headdress, relates to the cone of power the coven must raise. Male witches who are co-leaders of the coven sometimes wear a horned headdress to symbolize their relationship to the horned male consort of the Goddess. The horns may be of deer, goat or ram; it does not matter. Others, influenced by North American Indian Shamanism, may have a feathered headdress. Some witches wear the traditional witches' garter; others do not.

The object of special clothing is simple. It is firstly to wear clothes that are worn only when acts of magic are being performed; putting on these clothes conditions the wearer to a state of preparedness, and the clothes themselves, after long use, may carry an energy of their own. Secondly, clothes of particular colours may be worn for various celebrations or rituals. Green is proper for spring festivals; green is also a colour associated with the Goddess as Maid, and with her consort as God of the Woodland. The knight who challenged Gawain in the old romance was 'the Green Knight', and Robin Hood and his men wore Lincoln Green. Red, the colour of vitality, is also appropriate for a man; this tradition was adopted by the theatre, which frequently dresses the Devil in red. Other colours are used from time to time.

Rings, pendants and necklaces can take many forms, and each witch will make an individual choice. Obviously, pentagrams and hexagrams are common; so are emeralds and rubies and other red and green stones. Amber is popular, for it has or can be given considerable static electricity. Black stones are also popular, as are representations of the moon, either new or full.

On celebratory occasions, witches enjoy dressing up just as much as other people. Nevertheless, many contemporary witches, especially those who work alone or in very small groups, often wear quite usual clothes, because they feel comfortable in them and feel no necessity to dress up for the Goddess. Some, indeed, feel that to dress up for any but the most important and deliberately theatrical rituals is to suggest that the Old Religion is set apart from ordinary life, whereas it should permeate it and be a part of everything one does at work or at play.

44 *Are witches feminists?*

As it is no more easy to define feminism than witchcraft, this is not as straightforward a question as it seems.

Certainly all witches believe in the importance of revering birth and revere woman as the bringer-to-birth, and object to any society that places women in positions inferior to men. They are therefore passionately concerned that women should be given their proper role in society, that they should be regarded in law as the equal of men, that they should be considered the true heads of families and that motherhood should be rewarded by adequate maternal leave from work, and so forth.

On the other hand, many witches feel that some feminists adopt attitudes which are not in the spirit of the witch's law. Women who do not recognize that the harmony of nature demands recognition of the male contribution to life and the enhancement of life, and who see the Craft as entirely a woman's religion, are at fault. This does not mean that there should not be covens or groups entirely composed of women. One must, after all, have freedom of association; it does, however, mean that men must not be excluded from the religion on principle, and that, ideally, no coven should be wholly male-dominated or wholly female-dominated.

Some witches also feel that the role of woman as mother and home-maker is of supreme importance, and do not share their sisters' passionate conviction that women should work to achieve positions of power in the worlds of business and politics. They take the view that ultimately they would rather serve the Goddess than Mammon. Others, looking back upon the times when society was both matriarchal and matrilineal, feel it is important to work towards a social revolution and the overthrow of patriarchal and patrilineal systems.

Thus, as is true in most religions, there are different opinions about the role of the individual in society and about the shape society should take. Because of their creed, no true witch could subscribe to any totalitarian or tyrannical regime or accept any social system that did not take care of the old, the sick and the poor. Because of their own history of persecution, they are passionate supporters of the rights of minorities, especially where religion is concerned. In North America, therefore, they will often be found working for the rights of the native Indians. Because they reverence womanhood, they are opposed to any kind of pornography that denigrates women; they are not, however, opposed to eroticism, as they have no sense of sexual pleasures being anything but good.

These are all generalizations and therefore imprecise. There is no orthodoxy in witchcraft, and many true witches will interpret the demands of their religion differently.

45   Are there not many charlatans among witches?

The answer must be, sadly, 'yes', if one means by 'charlatan' a person who pretends to have skills and qualifications which he or she does not possess and who uses this pretence for self-glorification and for money. There are, however, several kinds of charlatan among witches, and they should perhaps be identified.

First there is the character who uses a public platform to present the Craft as if it were a combination of a consciousness-raising group and improvisational theatre. There is nothing wrong with getting together with other people and discussing one's private feelings, emotional difficulties and spiritual condition. It is often (though not, I fear, always) good therapy. Nor is there anything wrong with gathering people together and inciting them to dance, chant and act out various roles. This can be a great emotional release for many people and, again, good therapy, and such performances have formed a part of many religious gatherings. (One thinks of the fundamental Baptists, of the Holy Rollers and of the dance rituals of many tribes and cultures.)

The charlatanry exists not in doing this kind of thing but in suggesting that this kind of activity is central to the Craft, and that the kind of energy 'high' one gets by participating is the same as the 'high' one gets when creating a cone of power and doing necessary work. The heart of witchcraft is not the creation of mass enthusiasm or mass hysteria. Traditionally, all groups are no larger than thirteen, and it may well be that one of the reasons for meeting in such small groups is to avoid giving any single charismatic person the opportunity to become a spiritual demagogue.

Nevertheless, large meetings and celebrations have their place. No one should cavil at the organization of a large gathering in which there can be an exchange of views between people of different Craft traditions. I merely wish to emphasize that any person who suggests that such meetings are a central part of the Old Religion is giving a false impression.

Another kind of false witch is that person who, while celebrating all the sabbats, taking great pains to possess the paraphernalia he or she believes to be essential to the Craft, and wearing whatever pendants and rings seems proper, never actually does any work. There are a number of so-called witches who have splendid accoutrements and robes and who are learned in the literature of the Craft and in all things relating to paganism and the occult but who never utilize the power they possess. Some of these so-called witches say they are nervous of using magic, that they fear they might be unable to control themselves and might do damage to themselves or others. These people are not true witches. They do not practise what they preach, and do a disservice to the craft, for they are soon discovered to be little but show.

A third kind of false witch is the person who, calling himself or herself a witch, is in fact an occultist, a magician or wizard. These people ignore the nature-orientated aspect of the Old Religion, deal in terms of a complex hierarchy of spiritual forces, demons, angels and the like, make the kabbalah the centre of their religious universe, emphasize the importance of elaborate and lengthy rituals, and organize themselves, or are organized, into a hierarchical system. Magicians and wizards do have a religious system and do have power, for the power of doing magic, or what has been called sorcery, is peculiar to no single religion. They are, however, as far from being witches as are Catholics from being Taoists.

Finally, of course, and rather sadly, there are those people who, gifted with psychic sensitivity, call themselves witches because of this. They see clearly and far. They are most valuable people and, if they can survive the pressure of their own sensitivities and neither break down under the strain nor choose to repress their intuitions as being too uncomfortable to live with, they can do much good. They are not necessarily witches, however. Indeed, it is saddening to observe them claiming that title, when they have not yet found the spiritual support and strength a religious belief would give them and when they could clearly, with their abilities, be valuable members of the Craft community.

46   Is there a life-style peculiar to witches?

This is not an easy question to answer, as witches are highly individualistic and can be found in almost all walks of life and at all income levels. I can only make some general observations.

Witches are very much aware of the food they eat, for they not only attempt to live in harmony with the natural world but also celebrate the changing of the seasons with appropriate food and drink, and many are herbalists. Witches therefore tend to avoid junk food and to follow well-balanced diets. Their kitchens and their gardens contain more herbs than the average, and their medicine cupboards tend to include herbal and homeopathic remedies.

They are also aware of the way in which the home environment can either stimulate or inhibit sensitivity. As a consequence, the majority of witches' houses contain a good deal of bric-a-brac, especially small sculptures of the Goddess in her various guises, and of animals and birds. Their crockery usually includes a good many bowls, for bowls are reminders of plenitude and of fertility. Indeed, witches tend to enjoy ceramics particularly, for pottery is made from the earth itself and is a reminder of our connection with the physical world. Because for them time is an unending flow and they feel that they may well have experienced historical times in person, they tend to be addicted to antiques and collectibles that give them a sense of oneness with the past.

All this is of course, entirely apart from the objects and furnishings which are primarily related to their craft, and which differ considerably from household to household. Some witches collect spell boxes, and these may be displayed openly. Growing plants are, on the whole, preferred to cut flowers, and most witches have several potted plants about the house. Domestic pets are almost invariable. Witches are cat-lovers in general, but many witches also have dogs and birds.

There is, indeed, nothing particularly unusual about the life-style of the average witch. Few people entering a witch's home for the first time would be likely to notice much out of the ordinary, though, of course, there are exceptions.

47 Do witches make money?

In spite of all the charms and spells to acquire wealth presented in various catchpenny books on witchcraft, witches do not, in general, use their powers for personal gain but earn their bread, most usually, in other ways. They believe it to be proper to ask for money when there is a true necessity for it, or for some special purpose connected with the Craft, but only then.

Witches frequently, either individually or collectively, help others by way of their magic. They perform healing spells, remove curses, exorcise ghosts and practise the arts of reading the tarot, or other modes of divination. The general practice is to charge a set fee for a tarot or other kind of reading, for this is an established practice in other than witchcraft circles. The payment is regarded as being one for the time spent rather than the reading itself, and varies according to the length of the reading. This also applies to other work that some witches do, such as using their clairvoyant powers to assist the police (which happens more frequently than is generally supposed). When it comes to casting spells of healing, lifting curses and the like, it is common to charge no fee, though it is not uncommon for those who have been helped to give the witch a present of some kind a little time after the work has been completed and has been successful. Witches work for other witches without any reward.

Witches certainly never haggle over money. Nor do they take money from the poor. They may receive fees for lecturing or giving classes, as do others. In general, however, witchcraft is not a paying proposition.

48   How does one become a witch?

Many contemporary writers on witchcraft state that a person who cannot find another witch to perform a rite of initiation can perform a self-initiation rite. There are a number of books which give examples of self-initiation rites.

Others take a more traditional view and insist that one must be properly initiated by a witch, either alone or in a coven. Every coven has its own initiation ritual. Some involve ritual flagellation and nudity. Some do not. Some are elaborate; others are simple. There is no set pattern, save that in all cases the person initiated dedicates himself or herself to the service of the Goddess and to the true use of the Craft.

It is traditional that no coven recruits members. Nevertheless, a number of prominent witches do give lectures and courses on witchcraft which, quite obviously, have the effect of recruitment. It is traditional for a witch or a coven to be approached by the would-be witch and asked for initiation and, if the coven is in agreement or the witch agrees, for that initiation to take place approximately a year and a day from the time of the request, or when the would-be witch is twenty-one, if that is later. This wait is to ensure that the request was not frivolous and also to give time to study the would-be witch's attitude. Witches take initiation very seriously. The act of initiation is, indeed, less the giving of an entrance permit to an exclusive club than an act of recognition. One might say that only those who are witches already are initiated as witches.

Many people practise the Craft or part of it outside the boundaries of Wicca, for spell-power is not exclusive to witches. Some of these feel that a total commitment to Wicca is too heavy a burden. They also fear that, once their powers are increased by constant practice and by learning and studying with others, they may not be strong enough to resist the temptation to misuse them. They also cannot help being somewhat put off by all the anti-Wicca propaganda they have heard, and wonder what they might be getting into.

Much of Wiccan practice remains secret. In the past this was to protect witches from torture and death. Nowadays many witches feel that there are some matters of the craft which should not be allowed to fall into the hands of irresponsible or malicious people. Though a number of Books of Shadows have been published, it is noticeable that they do not provide anything like full information. Moreover, the vast majority of books on Wicca today deal almost entirely with Wiccan symbolism and rituals; they do not instruct their readers in the actual work of witches as spell-casters. The unfortunate consequence is that many people fail to understand that many witches feel the work to be just as important as the rituals, if not more so.

The would-be witch must learn the skills of the Craft and discover for what particular skills he or she has most aptitude. Worship without work is a car without a driver; it will not make the journey. Fortunately, however, the rituals themselves do provide the participant with power and make effective use of the power possible. It is when the would-be witch has discovered his or her power and has made good use of it that initiation becomes a possibility. Here I must emphasize the phrase 'good use'. The work done must have been done according to the witch's law which, while offering the freedom of 'Do what you will', also presents the duty of acting always in love and of harming no one.

Part II

Rituals and Celebrations

Introduction

The following rituals are quite different from those presented by Gardnerian and Alexandrian witches and, indeed, by all other pagan groups whose ceremonies have been published. This is because I have come to the belief that we need short, simple and immediately intelligible rituals in which the symbolism is clear, rather than ceremonies whose complexity may well defeat their object, which is to unite all members of the group both intellectually and emotionally.

Wicca is an old religion and had its origins in the worship of a Mother Goddess, who was also a trinity. Early believers worshipped this goddess under many names and in many cultures and made use of many symbols which today appear to be esoteric. If our ceremonies are made in terms of this ancient symbolism, combining many elements from past practices of different times and countries, we are in danger of losing the essential simplicities of all true worship. We are also in danger of placing our religious ceremonies upon a plane that is not the plane of our daily life. We must not keep our religion in a mental compartment separate from our ordinary concerns and become overly fascinated by detail and elaboration.

Wicca, like all religions, is syncretic. Just as the Jewish and Christian faiths gathered together beliefs and attitudes from many preceding faiths, so Wicca, in its twentieth-century revival, has brought together attitudes and symbols from many places. However, syncretism of this kind leads eventually to fragmentation. In the Christian Church the urge to simplify and clarify the complexities of theology has led, and continues to lead, to the creation of many different sects. These were labelled heretical by the Church of the past. In the present day, the term 'heresy' is used less frequently, but it is notable that there are many different kinds of Christianity, most of which arose from an impulse to return to fundamentals.

These rituals may well be regarded as a similar attempt to return to essentials. They differ, however, from some fundamentalist approaches in other religions in that they do not attempt to create a simple rule-book for human behaviour or to shape any kind of dogma. I myself regard them as foundations, so made that many different individual buildings may be erected upon them. Every witch will, and should, make and become his or her own temple, and the architecture will differ. For all this, I would suggest that whenever a ritual is held indoors the altar or round table at the centre of the circle should bear a figure of the Goddess, and either a single lit candle in a candlestick or, preferably, candles in a three (or four) branched candlestick. The four elements should also be represented, earth to the north, air to the east, fire to the south, and water to the west. Earth is usually represented by salt, and water, of course, by water. A burning stick of incense can represent both air and fire. Other implements and symbols may be included, according to the feelings of the celebrants or the nature of the particular occassion.

It is my belief that very few people indeed can keep up a high level of emotional and psychic intensity for very long. Lengthy, complicated ceremonies overtax the memory of the participants, so that they attend more to getting their lines correct than to entering into the worship. Moreover, very few people can cope with constantly changing attitudes within one ceremony. Therefore these rituals are short and simple, and each deals with only one main theme. In order to cover all the important themes of Wiccan beliefs and practices I have therefore felt obliged to add to the number of rituals listed in the calendar of what we might reasonably call mainstream traditions. I have added these rituals too for another reason. While many witches hold ceremonies or meet at the full of the moon, the majority seriously celebrate their religion only eight times during the year, on the sabbats. It is my belief that we should reinforce and reassert our religion a little more frequently. It is a long time between sabbats, and the full moon cannot be relied upon to occur midway between them.

In creating these rituals, I have made some use of Christian feast-days, just as the early Christian Church made use of the feast-days of the Old Religion. It is an act of partial reclamation. I have also followed the principles of the ancient menstrual calendar which was based on phases of the moon and which regarded the day as stretching from noon to noon, not midnight to midnight.

I have used the male pronoun more frequently than the female in these rituals because I myself am a male witch and therefore feel this natural. Moreover, it makes for intolerable clumsiness to say 'he or she' or 'she/he' in every sentence. The gender of the leader really does not matter, though some will feel very understandably that certain rituals ought to be led only by a woman.

1

Commencement Rituals

Introduction

When the group gathered to perform a ritual contains more than three or four people, it is useful to formalize the necessary gathering of energy, so that all are of one mind. In smaller groups this is less necessary on most occasions. If you are working alone, you may sometimes feel that a commencement ritual will help you; the Ritual of the Powers is so constructed that one person can perform it alone without discomfort.

When a group has been working together for some time, a commencement ritual may not be needed. There is no particular virtue in following a pattern-book. Nor does it matter if, during these rituals, people make small mistakes. The power of magic is not dependant upon mere verbal accuracy: it derives from intent, not linguistic precision. Those who tell us (as do some occultists) that a ritual will succeed only if all the participants are letter-perfect are simply preparing an explanation of failure in advance. This excuse is particularly easy to produce when the ritual is lengthy and elaborate, of course, and it has been suggested that the creators of some of the rituals of High Magic have had this in mind all along.

Making the Circle

This is a simple ritual. The leader of the group should gather the celebrants round the fire or the altar-table and, standing to the south of it, draw a circle around the company with his or her staff, wand, knife or sword, keeping himself within the circle and moving clockwise or deosil. He should complete the circle three times and end up to the south of the altar, facing north.

All rituals are held facing north, by tradition. The explanation may be that it was realized long ago that magical power is related to magnetic power and that therefore one should face the magnetic pole.

The leader does not need to speak aloud while making the circle, but if words are felt necessary, the following, or something similar, might be used:

First	I make this circle around us for love's protection and in the power of the first name of the Lady.
Second	I make this circle around us to join us together in the power of the second name of the Lady.
Third	I make this circle around us that is endless in reverence for the third name of the Lady.
Concluding	In the three names of the Lady the circle is made.

At the conclusion of the ritual, the leader should simply 'cut' an opening in the circle on the south side where he is standing and say 'The gate is open.' Then the company, moving clockwise, should leave the circle by that invisible gate.

Summoning Ritual

This is a very simple ritual indeed. The leader of the group should, after making the circle round the company and entering it himself, direct all present to imagine and feel energy flowing up into them from the centre of the earth. He should slowly describe the flow of the energy up through the legs, the thighs, the torso, to the shoulders, and then describe how it spreads out from the shoulder like branches of a tree, until the branches of all gathered in the circle are intertwined. He should then ask if everyone is ready. If anyone is not yet ready, the company must wait a little. Once all feel that the circle of energy is in place, the ritual may begin.

Ritual of the Powers

This is a ritual for commencing any ritual or work. The four powers of the magus (the master magician and seer of ancient Middle Eastern tradition) are 'to know' (Latin: nescere), 'to dare' (audere), 'to will' (velle) and 'to be silent' (tacere). These correspond with the four elements, air, water, fire, earth. In unity these four elements give rise to a fifth power, 'to go' (ire)— which is to say, to progress, to evolve, to make one's journey.

These can be seen as the five points of the pentagram, for the pentagram is made with five lines or movements. One ritual therefore consists of making the pentagram.

Place at the centre of your spell table, or in front of you in some way, a candle floating in a bowl of water or standing in water, around which salt has been placed, or actual earth together with salt if that is preferred. Facing north, the speaker should then draw the pentacle in the air with a wand or, if a wand is not used, with the forefinger. One line should be drawn for each of the first four lines of the verse, and one for the concluding couplet.

> I Know by the powers of Air;
> By the powers of Water I Dare;
> By Fire I wield my Will;
> By Earth I am Silent still,

> and in their heart and hight
> I tread my road aright.
>
> Blessed be!

This can, of course, be done by a witch alone, by a group leader or by several people in unison within the circle. The ritual maker or makers must face north. It can also be done by pacing the lines of the pentacle. There are many possible variations.

Ritual of the Watchers

The ritual of the Four Watchtowers is another commencement ritual. It is used in the Gardnerian tradition, at the creation of the circle, but is presented here without the hierarchical terminology of that tradition.

Leader: You who surround us,
            Guardians, Watchers,
            the dead we were and are
            and the unborn,
            help us, guide and bless us,
            for we are
            at one and one
            in spirit and in life.

[As the following words are spoken, the leader turns to the appropriate points of the compass, and bows his head, and the others, repeating the words, follow suit.]

> From the East bring us
> the powers of Air
>
> From the South bring us
> the tongues of Fire
>
> From the West bring us
> the singing of Water

From the North bring us
the wisdom of Earth

With you in holiness
of life perpetual
that is for us within
the name of the Goddess
we now rededicate the whole we are
in time and out of time.

All blessings be!

In the Celtic tradition the 'Four Airts' of the compass points are attached to the following colours : purple-red for the east, white for the south, blue-green for the west, and black for the north. Other traditions have different colour designations.

2

Sacra Privata

Introduction

'*Sacra Privata*' was the term given by the Romans to the private religious rites of a household, family or tribe. These must obviously vary considerably from family to family, or coven to coven. They differ from the sabbat rites in dealing directly with particular events in personal life. I have presented rituals for initiation, naming, handfasting, birth-blessing and passing from this life. In any coven or family, other rites may be needed from time to time. Many of these could be constructed around the various blessing spells I have given in the third part of this book.

I have not included a rite of exorcism as dealing with ghosts is a somewhat specialized activity and a thorough understanding of different kinds of psychic phenomena is needed if one is to do the work efficiently. Jean Kozakari and I did, however, include a full rite of exorcism in our book, *A Gathering of Ghosts* (Western Producer Prairie Books, 1989). Nevertheless, some spells to deal with the simpler forms of psychic disturbance are included in Part III of this book.

Initiation Ritual

In some traditions there are three grades of Wicca, and only witches of the second or third grade may initiate others. Some witches feel that this process leads towards the creation of ranks within the craft, and therefore towards a hierarchical structure of the kind found in occult societies such as the Order of the Golden

Dawn. I am myself of this opinion. Nevertheless, in any witch's life there are developments, which are recognized by his or her companions as well as by the witch, and it is proper for these developments to be recognized and signaled in some way. In this Book of Shadows (the conventional term for a witch's or a coven's collection of rites and spells), therefore, I offer both an initiation rite and a later rite of naming.

The initiation rite should be performed by another witch, a year and a day after the request has been made. It should be performed before two witnesses, who must be sympathetic but who need not be witches. Others may also be present if all parties desire it. It need not be performed within a circle; that is a matter for individual preference, but there should be symbols of the four elements earth, water, air and fire, present on the table or altar.

The initiate should bring to the gathering whatever implements he or she uses, as they are to be dedicated. If the initiate uses many implements, a small key selection should be brought; it is not, after all, practicable to cart along heavy spell tables or a large collection of spell boxes or bottles of philtres.

The ceremony should take place during the waxing of the moon or when the moon is full.

The name the candidate takes may be spoken aloud or remain unspoken and secret, the candidate saying it only to himself or herself.

Leader: This room is her room, this hour is her hour; these words and deeds are made in her, through her, the three-named and the myriad-named.

Candidate repeats after the leader: In her name and names I touch this salt; element of earth be strength in me.

In her name and names I touch this flame; element of fire make bright my spirit.

In her name and names I hold this air; element of air make sure my breath.

In her name and names I enter water; element of water cleanse my mind.

Earth, fire, air and water, in your presence I bow my head to everything that lives and is in her, of her, and shares her power as I share and serve her power of life.

Leader: Powers are duties. Do you now accept the burdens of the powers that she brings?

Candidate: I accept.

Leader: The power to speak with spirits.

Candidate: I accept.

Leader: The power to find that which is hidden.

Candidate: I accept.

Leader: The power to understand the voices on the wind.

Candidate: I accept.

Leader: The power to change water into wine.

Candidate: I accept.

Leader: The power to perceive truth in the cards.

Candidate: I accept.

Leader: The power to heal the body and the mind.

Candidate: I accept.

Leader: The power to change ugliness to beauty.

Candidate: I accept.

Leader:	The power to bless, to bind, to ban, to curse.
Candidate:	I accept.
Leader:	And do you accept these powers in love and trust?
Candidate:	I do.
Leader:	And do you accept the rule: Love and harm no-one?
Candidate:	I do.
Leader:	Have you the courage for the ordeal?
Candidate:	I do.

[A blindfold is affixed by one of the witnesses.]

Leader:	There is a place of darkness all must know. You have known that darkness. know it now. You walk through darkness. Darkness is of her as is the day, as are sun, moon and stars and every thing that swims or crawls or flies or roots in earth or lives within the mind, as pain is hers and happiness. Do you in darkness no accept her dark?
Candidate:	I do.

[The blindfold is taken off by one of the witnesses.]

Leader:	And do you now accept the light?
Candidate:	I do.
Leader:	Here are the implements you use. Oil on your finger, touch each to her service, saying, 'This I dedicate to her and all other implements I may use.'

Candidate says as he/she touches each implement:	This I dedicate to her and all other implements I may use.
Candidate:	I dedicate these implements and myself to her service and I bind myself To study and pursue the Craft, To use the Craft in love and for the good, To keep the feasts, To hide what should be hidden, To witness to whatever should be shown, To love, to seek the truth, in all my days. I put my name to this. One name is known and it is............... One name is now become my name and this I do not speak but place it in her hands.
Leader:	In her, through her, I bless your ways and days. You are now of the Craft. Blessed be!
All present:	Blessed be!

Naming Ritual

During the initiation ceremony the witch has taken a Wiccan name which may or may not be a secret one. There comes a time, however, when a witch may feel that he or she should have a name for general use in Craft meetings or even for public use, and this should not be the secret witch name, for the secret name is used only privately. It is good, therefore, to name a person by means of a different rite.

Another use of the naming ceremony is in the naming of a newborn child, and exactly the same ceremony may be used, though the child should be held by the mother throughout and then lifted to touch the foreheads of the name-giver and the witnesses. A name given to a baby may need to be added to or changed when the child is full grown. There is no reason why one name may not be added to another. After all, the children of royalty are usually given a number of names, only one of which they choose to use in public, and this may not be the one used by friends. (King Edward VIII was known as David to his family and friends, for example.)

The leader, or name-giver, should stand within the circle and face the person receiving the name, who may be either alone or attended by two other witches. Other members of the group may stand outside the circle. The four elements should be represented on a table within the circle, and there should be three candles, preferably in a three-branched candlestick. When each element is mentioned in the penultimate verse, the name-giver should touch the symbol of the element with a wand, and when the name is given, the wand should be touched to the third eye of the person being named.

Name-giver: It is the time for naming.
I name the sea.
It is the place of bearing,
the place of birth,
the depth of depth,
the cradle of the moon.
I name the moon.
It is her word, her name.

It is the time for naming.
I name the earth.
It is the place of hiding,
the place of growth,
the dark of dark,
the riddle of our love.
I name our love.
It is her love, her name.

It is the time for naming.
I name the wind.
It is the way of movement,
the way of breath,
the sound of sound,
the power of the song.
I name the song.
It is her song, her name.

It is the time for naming.
I name the fire.
It is the place of wisdom,
the place of fear,
the choir of choirs,
the unending vision.
I name the vision.
It is her, her name.

This is the time of naming,
I name your name.
I spell the name in
Earth, Air, Water, Fire
and through her, in her;
This name is named

....
in time, and out of time.
0, blessed be!

The named one should then kiss the name-giver upon the forehead, and also the two witnesses. The ceremony concludes with the opening of the circle, or the ceremony may continue with the following birth blessing, if the naming is of a newborn child or infant.

Birth Blessing

As witches do not believe in original sin, there is no need to purify a newborn child by a religious rite, as some Christians believe. Although there are various rites for what has been misnamed witch baptism, I do not consider them valid. I do not think it ethical to dedicate another human life to a religion of which it can have no understanding. In any case, every child born is born to the Goddess, and dedication is therefore unnecessary. It is, however, proper to bless a newborn child. It seems, indeed, if we are to accept the evidence of folk-tales, that in the past a birth was always attended by a blessing. There are many stories of blessing gifts being offered at a birth and, though fairy stories often include a gift of evil or hardship from the third of three fairies or godmothers, this is no more than an indication that the story recalls the Triple Goddess, one of whose faces is that of death. The three gifts of the magi in the story of Christ also support the view that blessing gifts were an accepted ritual, and there are other stories of birth gifts in myths of many cultures. Child-blessing was very important to families in the past, when infant mortality was high and only a small number of children survived their first few years.

> In the name of Truth,
> In the name of Light,
>
> In the name of Love,
> the Three of Power,
>
> I bless this child
> with strength of limb,
>
> I bless this child
> with strength of soul,
>
> I bless this child
> with truth of heart,
>
> I bless this child
> with ease of mind,
>
> I bless this child
> with keen strong speech,

I bless this child
with perfect hearing,

with love, with grace,
with understanding,

and by the power
of Love, Light, Truth

protect his days
and all his ways.

This spell may be cast either by one person or by a group of
people standing in a circle around the child's crib, the leader
speaking the first stanza, and the other stanzas being spoken in
turn by each member of the group, proceeding clockwise, the
whole company repeating each stanza after the speaker. The last
two stanzas should be spoken in unison.

Handfasting (Marriage)

A witch marriage is called a handfasting. It should take
place at noon, for noon is the ending of one day and the beginning
of another. If possible, it should be held out of doors, and if it can
be held in the spring, preferably in April, so much the better. The
bride should wear something green, and the groom something
crimson. The bride's jewellery should include silver, and the
man's gold, for silver is the colour of the moon and the Goddess,
and gold is the colour of the sun and of the consort-king.

In this ceremony, there is no handfaster or authority figure.
The two people have the authority of their own decision, and the
handfasting is made in terms of their unity within the natural
world and their dedication to the Goddess.

If desired, music may be played during the gathering of the
company into the circle and during the dance. Ideally, the music
should be folk-music, pipe and fiddle, but this does not matter.

The company forms a circle, the bride and groom among
them. At the bride's signal, she is led by women under a canopy
in the centre of the circle. This, if outdoors, can be made of a

bedsheet draped over poles. It should be open-sided, so that all can see the couple. A huge beach-umbrella could be used, and if it has to be held, it will have to be held by the bride. If bad weather forces the ceremony to take place indoors, the design of the canopy is up to the ingenuity of the participants.

The bride, facing north, calls the groom to join her with the words:

Bride: My hand is yours;
              your hand is mine;
              I welcome you into
              this my temple.

[The groom comes forward and joins her under the canopy.]

Groom: My hand is yours;
              Your hand. is mine.
              We are the temple.

[They stand together, hand in hand, and kiss. The bride gives the groom one half of an apple, cut transversely, to reveal the pentagram pattern made by the seeds.]

Bride: I am your nourishment.
              You are mine.
              We are the feast.

Groom: I am your nourishment.
              You are mine.
              We are the feast.

[They each take a ritual bite out of their halves of the apple and bury the remainder in an already prepared hole. The bride says to the groom:]

Bride: Give me your name.

Groom: ....

Bride: Your name is within me.

Groom: Give me your name.

Bride: ....

Groom: Your name is within me.

Bride: In love and trust.

Groom: In love and trust.

Bride: We are air.
         It rings us round.

         [She walks round the groom, deosil.]

Groom: We are fire.
       It rings us round.

       [He walks round the bride, deosil.]

Bride: We are water;
         It rings us round.

         [She walks round the groom]

Groom: We are earth;
       It rings us round.

       [He walks round the bride.]

Together: We are the circle's heart, the centre,
              and the heart of the pulse of life,
              and the servants of the Goddess;
              in her, through her, we live and breathe
              and have our loves and understandings.
              As she wills, so must it be.

[They step forward out of the canopy, and the company dances around them, the men deosil and the women widdershins, with hands joined. They dance round three times, and then stop, turn to the centre and raise their hands crying:

All: Blessed be!

[To which the handfasted couple respond:]

Couple: Blessed be!

The handfasting concludes with feasting.

Rite of Passage (Funeral Ceremony)

A burial ritual is not necessary in witchcraft, nor is a cremation ritual. We do not need to address ourselves to the problem of disposing of mortal remains, though it is pleasing to scatter a person's ashes in a fashion he or she would have appreciated and in an appropriate place, and it is good to plant or place flowers on a grave as a symbol of life's vitality and continuance.

We should, however, concern ourselves with the passing of the spirit through the gate into another dimension, and we should help ease that passage. This ritual should therefore be spoken soon after death, either over the body or in the place where the body died, if possible. If this is not possible, the message can still be sent by envisaging the person you wish to help. This ritual can be performed alone or in a group and is composed so that it can be either spoken by one person or delivered in a circle.

If it is a group ritual, the altar or table should carry three white candles and the usual symbols of earth, water and air, the lit candles to symbolize fire. If desired, symbols of passage may be added to reinforce the intent of the group, such as a model of a ship. The ship of death, laden with a dead person's goods and with provisions for a journey, is found in both Egyptian and Scandinavian cultures, as well as in many others. Indeed, if so desired, this ritual can take place on a sea shore, and the model of a burning ship can be sent out on the tide.

Leader: You waited for birth
and you were born.
You found your springtime
and grew tall.
You walked the summer
of fulfillment.
You neared the gateway
in your fall,
and now you are taken
by the hand
through the gateway
that is death,
upon a further path
a further
gathering of
the spirit's breath.

Leader, and   Be easy on your journey;
then all,   good is with you.
verse by
verse   Here is strength
to help you on your journey.

Feel love in your journey.
Our love is in you.

We send our love within you
through the gate.

Have faith upon your journey
bright with truth.

You are released from
the fetters of this time,
You are released
and freed to make your journey.

You have our happiness
at your release.

Look forward, forward,
and step out upon
this new bright path.
We bless your every footstep

in and through the power
of our Lady,

Who is life perpetual
and who leads

you onwards and away
from us, our time,

the small house of our time,
our little time,
from which we too
will move upon our journeys.

Goddess be with you,
as with us.

Fare well.

3

A Witch's Calendar

Introduction

The following calendar has been constructed according to a number of principles.

If one is to keep one's religion in mind throughout the year, one needs fairly frequent reminders of its duties. Moreover, one must 'keep in touch' with the Power regularly. This is difficult if one is not a professional lecturer on the subject or a constant attender at pagan or Wiccan conferences. Ideally, not more than twenty-eight days should pass between ceremonies, and at some periods of the year more frequent ceremonies may be needed.

There are a number of feast-days in the year that have been celebrated for more years than the Christian religion has existed, if one is to put any credence in folk-memory. Some of these have been Christianized, some not, although every day in the year now has one or more saints' names attached to it. Thus we should celebrate not only the equinoxes and solstices but also other days.

Wicca is concerned with the enhancement of human life, and all important aspects of it must be touched upon in Wiccan rituals. Thus there should be rituals devoted to consideration of children, of the old and of those who are persecuted for whatever reason. The various aspects of the Goddess must also be celebrated, and there must be ceremonies devoted specifically to each of the elements of air, earth, water and fire.

Every witch and every coven is likely to have special interests and concerns, and these may be celebrated in rituals peculiar to that coven or witch. They may, therefore, pick other days for their calendar and perhaps reclaim for Wicca other Christian (or Mohammedan or Buddhist) feasts. Witches in the Antipodes would certainly have to construct a different calendar: one can hardly celebrate a midwinter festival on a night of blazing heat or have a harvest ceremonial in the depths of winter. Witches living in the tropics must also think in terms of a different calendar. The one I present is for the temperate countries of the northern hemisphere and is adjusted to the climates with which I am most familiar.

Wicca is an individualist religion. All witches or covens should be prepared to create rituals to suit their own environment and their own backgrounds.

A Witch's Calendar

31 October-1 November	*A sabbat: Samhain*
21-2 November	Musemass
20-1 December	*A sabbat: Yule*
24-5 December	Modranect
15-16 January	Skillfest
31 January-1 February	*A sabbat: Brigid's Day*
28 February-1 March	Hearthday
20-1 March	*A sabbat: Alban Eilir*
31 March-1 April	Vertmass
30 April-1 May	*A sabbat: Beltaine*
29-30 May	Memory Day
23-4 June	*A sabbat: Midsummer*
19-20 July	Sunfest
31 July-1 August	*A sabbat: Lammas*
12-13 August	Diana's Day
24-5 August	Day of Tides
20-1 September	*A sabbat: Alban Elfed*
11-12 October	Eldmas

Of these feasts only the sabbats are observed by the generality of witches.

I have included one feast whose date is moveable. This is the Christian feast of Easter, which takes place on the first Sunday after the first full moon following the spring equinox. The name

Easter was taken from the pagan goddess Eostre, which is a variation on the name Astarte. I have therefore renamed, or re-spelt, this feast Eostre.

A Sabbat: Samhain (31 October - 1 November)

Hallowe'en takes places on 31 October and is the old Celtic feast of Samhain. It is a feast of the dead and was Christianized as All Hallows' Eve, the eve of All Saints' Day. It is a fire festival in recognition of the end of the summer and the beginning of winter. In ancient Manx and Irish tradition, Hallowmas was regarded as the beginning of a new year.

After sunset, and preferably at around nine o'clock in the evening, take an earthenware bowl and bury it up to the rim in the ground. Place salt in the bowl, and set in the salt a candle which should be short enough for the flame to be below the level of the earth. Each celebrant or, if preferred, the leader only, should have a glass or chalice of red wine in the hand. The celebrants should gather round the jar and say quietly:

> Blessings be upon the dead that know.
> Blessings be upon the dead that guard.
> Blessings be upon the dead that are.

This should be said in unison three times, and then the leader should say:

> In the name of goodness and mercy
> and the holy power
> grant your protection and guidance
> through this year,
> bless this house and household
> with your wisdom,
> bless this house and household
> with your strength,
> bless this house and household
> with your good.
>
> Answer if it be your will to answer.

There should then be a moment or two of silence, during which the candle flame may or may not respond by flickering. After this pause, whether or not the flame has flickered, the leader should say:

> Blessings upon you all in all ways we can bless.
> Gratitude for all good you have given.
> Reverence for all your help and guidance.
> This we say on this night of the year
> as token for all nights of all our years.

He should then say three times: 'Blessing be!' The celebrants should repeat the words after him.

Red wine should then be poured in the earth around the jar and a little in the jar, not enough to dowse the candle. The candle should be left to go out of its own accord, and the following morning the contents of the bowl should be buried in an appropriate place.

If this ceremony has to take place indoors, the bowl should be placed in the middle of a circle on the floor or in the centre of a round table, and the candle should be set in earth which is then covered with salt. As this is essentially a ritual of blessing upon the household, it may be that apartment-dwellers will have to perform it indoors or lose touch with the central intent of the work.

Musemass 21-2 November

In the Christian Church this is the day of St Cecilia, who may or may not have existed in fact but who has been regarded since the sixteenth century as the patron saint of music, because the fifth-century legend of St Cecilia states that, as the organ was playing for her marriage, she 'sang' (in her heart) to the Lord and prayed to remain a virgin, which she did. Paintings of her often show her with an organ or some other musical instrument, and both Dryden and Milton wrote poems in celebration of music on her feast-day. She is clearly a Muse figure, an inspirer, and can reasonably be associated with the nine Muses of Ancient Greece, who were originally a triad. Music (sacred music, that is) was acceptable to the early Church, as poetry was not. (Poets were not permitted to receive communion until the thirteenth century, according to some sources.) As music and dance and poetry are emphatically central to the religion of Wicca, it seems proper to celebrate this day. After all, in changing a saint's day into a day of the Goddess, we are only reversing the process initiated by the early Church.

Leader: Maiden, Mother, Wise One,
　　　　Goddess, Lady,
　　　　let your threefold grace
　　　　enfold our spirits
　　　　and grant us threefold vision,
　　　　threefold truth,
　　　　that we may praise
　　　　life's radiance in your ways.
　　　　Sing in our minds and spirits.
　　　　Bring us song.

All:　　Sing! Sing!

Leader: Move in our souls and bodies that we dance.

All:　　Dance! Dance!

Leader: Breathe your breath
　　　　through our breath
　　　　that poetry comes.

All:　　Let poetry come!

Leader: Fill us with understanding
　　　　so we may teach.

All:　　Teach! Teach!

Leader: Give us compassion
　　　　so that we may bless

All: Bless! Bless!

Leader: And, Goddess,
            let your sacred living light
            possess us with
            divine imagination,
            that in all ways of yours
            we make, renew.

All: Make! Renew!

Leader and These powers are ours
then all: by you, in you, through you.

Leader and Sing! Dance! Let poetry come!
then all: Teach! Bless! Make new!

Leader: Now in this day that
            is your threefold day
            of inspiration,
            bring us inspiration.
            Inspire, inspire, inspire!

All: Inspire! Inspire! Inspire!

Leader: That we may make life
            radiant in ourselves
            and for all others
            praising still your name.

All: We praise! We praise! We praise!

Leader and All blessings be!
then all:

A Sabbat: Yule (20-1 December)

Yule is the midwinter festival. It takes place at the winter
solstice when the sun enters Capricorn. The generally accepted

date is 21 December but purists may adjust the date according to the sun's position. The name 'Yule' is derived from the Old Norse word *iul*, which means a wheel, and refers to the notion of the year as a wheel turning through the seasons, the spokes being the equinoxes, the solstices and the great feasts of the quarter days. The ancient Celtic or druidic name for Yule is 'Alban Arthan'. The Romans celebrated the feast under the name 'Saturnalia'. (Saturn is the ruler of Capricorn.)

The feast is basically in celebration of the rebirth of the sun, the day when the sun, at its weakest, begins again to strengthen.

Traditional midwinter observances include lighting fires both outside and inside houses and decorating houses with holly, ivy, mistletoe, bay, rosemary and branches of box trees.

This celebration may be carried out in the open air around a bonfire or inside the house, standing in a circle, preferably around a circular table, which may, if it is desired, have a centrepiece of traditional greenery. Each person should hold a lighted candle or torch. If the celebration takes place outside, the candles or torches should be thrown into the fire at the end of the ceremony. If it takes place indoors, the candles should be placed in the centre of the round table, on a plate, and allowed to burn out naturally. The leader begins the rite, saying:

Leader: This night once more
the wheel begins
the turning year
of the whole

that is of Earth,
Air, Water, Fire,
that is of Body
and of Soul,

that is of all
that lives above,
below, within,
and near and far,

that is of Sun
and of the Day,
that is of Night
and Moon and Star

103

and all the Names
and all the Words
and all the breath
of all that breathes

and that has breathed
all life, all life,
and all is Life
and is the Wheel
that turns again.

[The celebrants start moving clockwise around the table or the bonfire.]

Chorus: We bless the turn

Leader: that turns again.

Chorus: We praise the turn

Leader: that turns again

Chorus: We bless the turn
in her Name
and through ours
in her
we bless

The ceremony is now concluded, and the celebrants should refresh themselves either upon traditional midwinter food and drink, such as mulled ale, mince-pies, rich cake, pork, ham and, as in every celebration, wholemeal bread, or upon whatever takes their fancy.

Modranect 24-5 December

This is the Saxon name for the night of Christmas Eve and means 'the Night of the Mother', or 'of mothering'. It has also been called, in Latin, 'Matrum Noctem'. It is not only another

celebration of the birth of the sun at the winter solstice: it is also a
day dedicated to the Goddess as Astarte. The day following the
Night of the Mother was devoted to the goddess as Sea-Mother,
and the image of the Goddess was launched out to sea on that
day. It was also a time for the giving of gifts. The Christmas tree
was originally a pine taken from the sacred grove of the Goddess,
and the decorations originated in the figures of subsidiary local
deities placed in the branches, as well as in the feast of lights
which takes place at this solstice time, to encourage the sun's
rebirth and the renewing of day.

If the house possesses a decorated Christmas tree, the celebrants should stand before it in a semi-circle. If it is a table-top
tree, they can stand around it. If the household does not have a
Christmas tree, as such, the celebrants should stand around some
other plant on which decorations have been placed.

Leader: This is the night of the mother,
the night of birth.

This is the night of giving
The gift of breath.

This is the night of drinking
the wine of life.

This is the night of blessing
the turning earth.

This is the night of welcoming
warmth in the heart.

[They lift their glasses of wine and drink. Each person says, in
turn:]

With this breath I speak
the word of love.

With this wine
I praise the wine of life.

105

With these hands I bless
the earth I love.

With all my heart I welcome
all her gifts,

and this gift I place
upon the tree.

[Each one places, or hangs, a gift or decoration on the tree.]

Leader and then all:	Blessings upon this household and all here. Blessings upon all our friends and comrades. Blessings upon all those who are our kindred.

[Now everyone speaks the name of any person they wish to bless, and it is repeated by all.]

Leader: This day we give and we receive her blessing.
Blessed be!

All: Blessed be!

Skillfest, 15-16 January

This day is the feast-day of St Henry of Coquet Island, a Dane who settled on this island off the coast of Britain in the twelfth century and, despite all argument, decided to remain there rather than return to Denmark. He was noted particularly for his tending of his garden, and also for his abilities in prophecy, divination and telekinesis. He died in 1127. Though Henry was an actual man and clearly a devout Christian, his day seems an appropriate one on which to celebrate and increase the gifts of perception and the psychic powers he possessed.

Leader and then all, verse by verse:	This day we call the power down to strengthen us in all our skills. We call by moon, we call by sun we call by air, earth, water, fire

We call by body, mind and spirit,
we call by flesh and bone and blood.

We call by each one of our senses
through which we see, touch, taste, smell, hear

and in the unity of the Goddess
that is, and brings, all powers to all

Leader: that our eyes read all signs, and see
in hands, cards, runes, coins,crystals, sands,
flames, coals, pools, clouds, shadows, grass,
leaves, flowers, fruit, bones, pebbles, stones
and every signature of life,
the sentence that the mind must find.

Leader and   This power we call into us
then all: and this skill.

Leader: And that our hands may find by touch
the hurt to heal, and heal the hurt,
and that our hands may have the power
to send the power to do good.

And that our hands may have the cunning
to know and shape the shapes we need
in air, in fire, in earth, in water,
and move always into blessings.

Leader: This power we call into us
then all: and this skill

And that our ears may hear in air,
in speech, in music, in all sound
the inner meanings of the sound,
and know the secrets of all sound.

Leader and   This power we call into us
then all: And this skill.

Leader: And that our will may have the power
to bless, to bind, to ban, to curse,
to heal, to teach and to transform
within the radiance of the Lady.

Leader and   This power we call into us
then all,   and this skill
verse by   upon this day and upon all our days;
verse: so may we be her instruments and she
within us our irradiated life.

So are these powers
within us,

Blessed be!

A Sabbat: Brigid's Day (31 January - 1 February)

The calendar gives 1 February as the feast of St Brigid, who
is a Christianized version of Brigid or Bride, the great Celtic
Mother Goddess. The Irish called the day Imbolc or Oimelc, and
it was a feast to celebrate the Triple Goddess and, to use Robert
Graves' phrase, 'the quickening of the year'. The Christian Church
considers 2 February the feast of the Purification of the Virgin
Mary. It is also called Candlemas, because altar candles are
blessed on that day.

On the eve of 1 February place a bed of hay or straw near the
front door of your house or apartment and beside it a chalice of
red wine, a wooden club and a biscuit or slice of cake. Before
going to bed, or at midnight, the members of the household
should gather at the front door and, after opening the door, say in
unison, three times:

Bride is coming. Bride is come.
Welcome Brigid to this home.

The following morning the wine should be poured and the
biscuit or cake crumbled at the foot of whatever statue, bush or
tree you regard as belonging to and essentially representing the
Goddess.

On the morning of 1 February, preferably as dawn is breaking, make a circuit of your garden, proceeding clockwise in general but making sure that no part of it is ignored. If you have no garden, make a similar circuit of all the plants in your house or apartment saying:

> This is the quickening
> of the year.
> Tuber and seed and root quicken
> into the coming of the light
> into the growing of the year.
>
> This is the quickening
> time of life.
> Root and seed and tuber quicken
> in your darkness
> in your waiting
> quicken into burgeoning life.
>
> This is the quickening
> of the time of love.
> Seed and root and tuber quicken,
> gather strength in love and praise,
> and blessed be!

If the garden is entirely invisible under snow, you should simply imagine, or remember, where the plants are. If the weather makes a trip outside hazardous, you may simply make the blessing from your threshold or even through the window. Eye-contact with the growing-place is necessary, however. Those who wish to conflate Brigid's Day with Candlemas and the Feast of the Purification of the Virgin Mary, may perform these rituals on the first and second of February.

Hearthday 28 February - 1 March

This is the day of Vesta, the matriarchal Roman goddess who guarded the temple hearth, and her followers, the Vestals, who kept alight the perpetual fire on the hearth and altar. The

Goddess looked after the household gods, to whom a Vestal had originally given birth. The household, symbolized traditionally by the hearth, is central to Wicca. It is therefore proper to devote one of the Wiccan ceremonies to the hearth and all it means to us.

The celebrants should gather round the fire in a semi-circle. If there is no fire in the house, they should gather round a fat red candle. A cauldron should be placed before the fire or be used to hold the burning candle. The table, or hearth, should also bear a plate containing bread and other food. A broom should be also among the accoutrements, as well as a dish of salt, and a wooden spoon. If the ceremony takes place before the fire, the mantelpiece or a small table can be used rather than the floor.

Leader: Maiden, Lady, Mother of us all,
we gather at the hearth within this house
to celebrate the strength that feeds us, heals us,
guards us, warms us, clothes us, gives us good.

Here we remember
and call up the power
of giving shelter
and of giving warmth.

All: Grant us the power.

Leader: Here we remember
and call up the power
of giving comfort
and of giving strength

All: Grant us the power.

Leader: Here we remember
and call up the power
of giving welcome
and of giving trust.

All: Grant us the power.

110

Leader: Protect this house now
and all of this household.

All: Protect this house now
and all of this household.

Leader: Keep the hearth good
and free of every harm.

All: Keep the hearth good
and free of every harm.

Leader: It is your hearth
and it is through your power
we live and work
and know you in our being

We are given strength here
at your hearth.

All: We are given strength.

Leader: We are given power
at your hearth

All: Your power is in us.

Leader: Maiden, Lady, Mother of us all,
here at this hearth
we celebrate and bless
the good of house and home.
This is our home,
and this our blessing.

All: Blessed, blessed be.

The ceremony over, the company should eat and drink together. If there is only one celebrant, it is only necessary to change the pronouns throughout from 'we' to 'I'.

A Sabbat: Alban Eilir (20 - 1 March)

The spring equinox takes place on 21 March, which is usually regarded as the first day of spring. The druids called this day 'Alban Eilir'. It should be the day on which the sun enters the sign of Aries, and purists may therefore use a more accurate date.

Place an earthenware bowl in the centre of a circle or round table and fill it three-quarters full of fresh water. Gather around the table. Each celebrant should have a smooth white pebble and a small bunch of spring flowers— just two or three blossoms. The leader begins by saying:

> Farewell to winter.
> Turn the wheel.

The leader should then take a pace to the left, as should all, as they repeat the words.

> Here is your memory
> and your promise.

He places a white pebble in the bowl. The person to his immediate left should then follow suit, the words being repeated by all, and the second pebble placed in the bowl. When all the pebbles are in the bowl, the leader should say:

> This day the promise
> is fulfilled.
> Hand and flower
> thank and bless.

The leader should then place flowers in the water. The other celebrants then place their flowers in the water with the same words. Then the leader should say:

> In the heavens and in earth
> this is beginning
> this is birth.

> In all that creep, walk,
> swim and fly,
> here is newness
> here is day,
>
> and here the Lady
> in her pride
> comes in kindness
> to our need.

The leader should then cup a hand into the water and drink from the hand saying:

> Dancing water,
> here divine
> is birthtime and
> her secret wine
> which here we share
> in love and praise
> that she may guide us
> in our ways.

All should then drink water in the same manner, and then move a second step to the left. After which the leader should say simply: 'Blessed be!' and this should be repeated by all in unison.

The water in the bowl should then be sprinkled, by hand, upon plants, upon the earth, upon growing things. When only the pebbles are remaining, they should be taken up and placed in a linen bag or wrapping and put away until there is another occasion to use them.

A meal, including milk and eggs, should then be shared; the tablecloth should be green.

Vertmass 31 March - 1 April

'Vertmass' means 'feast of green'. 1 April has long been called 'All Fools' Day'. In past times it was associated with 'Green George', the figure of the Goddess's consort as the Green King of the woodland, who in different times and places was also known as Herne or Green Jack. 'The Fool of Love' is another term for this figure who also turns up on May Day and is celebrated by making green men out of twined grasses or painting them on paper. This day is therefore devoted to notions of greenness, of spring, of new growth and of love. A relic of the old pagan view of the day beginning and ending at noon is revealed by the custom of stating that nobody can make anybody else an 'April Fool' after noon of 1 April which is to say, after the end of the day.

If this ceremony is held outdoors, it should take place before sunset, and the company should gather around a tree or a shrub. If it is held indoors, the central table or altar should carry a green candle or candles. The celebrants should all wear green and, if possible, carry a twig of fresh green foliage and spring flowers.

Leader: Remember that we move
from light to light,
the sudden shine of birth,
of death, the light
from day through night to day,
that we descend
into the dark and rise
up from the dark,
learned in dream and
deeper dreams than dream.

Remember that we move
from spring to spring,
from wakening towards
wakening.

All: This thrust of green
lay in the seed of winter.

Leader: Remember that we
move from birth to birth,
each moment, and each day,
week, month, and year,
through century upon
century, aeon on aeon.

All: The child of morning
           leaps up from the night.

Leader: This is a day to
           lift our hands to mornings,
           to wakenings of the seed,
           to acts of love
           that wake the seed
           and bring the green of April.

All: Desire and folly
           dance out from the dark.

Leader: Let us walk in green
           woods of the truth.

All: Truth, come into us
           in this beginning!

Leader: Let us dance
           the green paths of desire.

All: Desire, wake in us,
           in this beginning!

Leader: Let us sing
           the songs of springing leaves.

All: Trust uphold us
           in our new beginnings!

Leader: And let us carry
           the spring flowers of folly
           that are the joy and innocence
           she brings
           and with the
           clarities of children bless
           all children
           with beginnings.

All: Blessed be!

Eostre

Eostre (who may be related to the Greek Eos, the Dawn Goddess) is mentioned in the Anglo-Saxon epic, *Beowulf,* where it seems that she was identified with a goddess of the Ganges, most probably Kali. Her name is also one form of Astarte. The name 'Easter' was given to the Christian festival in the later Middle Ages. Red Easter eggs were placed on graves in Russia to assist rebirth. In England, this feast was once called the Hye Tide. Eggs and apples both featured in old ceremonies, and the Easter Bunny is a very ancient animal indeed.

On the eve of Eostre (Easter Saturday night), a table should be laid out with red candles, salt, water and a symbol of air (perhaps a glass or crystal ball), and the Eostran symbols of a red egg, an apple and a model or picture of a hare (or rabbit).

Leader: Dark before light;
         we sleep and wake.
         We descend into darkness;
         we rise at dawn.
         We bury the seed,
         and the seed awakens.
         Through night, through day,
         we die and are born.

Leader and   Birth is waiting for us.
then all,   It is coming.
verse by
verse: Birth is nearing us.
                The birth is near.

                This night of the year
                is every night.

                This moment and all moments
                birth is near.

Leader: And in this moment now
as in all moments
in the power of the Goddess Mother
we are born again.

All:　We are born again.

Leader: To life renewed and sacred
we are born.

All:　Blessings upon all powers
of renewal,
upon all making new,
on all new things
that brighten living with
a fresh made radiance.

Leader: So this we bless.

All:　We bless. We bless.

Leader: All blessed be!

All:　　All blessed be!

A Sabbat: Beltaine (30 April - 1 May)

The feast of Beltaine, 1 May, is an ancient European fire festival and also the Christian festival of Roodmas. Traditional practices are dancing around the maypole and the election of a May Queen.

On May Eve a fire should be made in a circular hearth outside. If the ceremony must take place inside, a lit candle set in a circle on the floor or on a round table will suffice. All celebrants should wear some fresh green twig from a deciduous tree, and mayblossom should be placed on the threshold of the house. The leader should begin.

Leader: Lady, this day
        is the day of shining;
        leaf and shoot and bud
        are new.
        Lady, this day
        is newly made,
        water and earth and
        air and fire
        in your hands as a
        flower opening,
        a bird singing,
        a child new born.

        Lady of kindness
        bless all kind;
        here we tread
        the tread of spring.

[The celebrants should then move round the circle, clock wise.]

All: Here we tread
     the tread of spring.

[If these words can be chanted or sung to tin whistle or flute, so much the better].

Leader: In our hearts you
        make us new.

All: The name is new,
[still   the name is new.
moving]

Leader: In our minds
        you give us light.

All: The name is light,
     the name is light

Leader: In our spirits we rejoice.

All: Lady, Lady, we rejoice.

[As the celebrants cease circling, the leader should then say:]

Leader: This is the spring
        of this and every
        year that is
        and every day,
        and every hour
        and every minute,
        this is the infinite
        of day.

        Here in beginnings,
        Lady, here
        bless and be kind,
        be thanked and bless,
        that the green shoot shoot
        and the life increase
        in strength and love
        this day and all.

All: And strength and love
         in every soul.

Leader, Blessed be!
then all:

After this, all the celebrants should eat and drink together.

Memory Day (29-30 May)

30 May is dedicated to Joan of Arc, who was burned as a heretic in Rouen market-place on that date in 1431. Whether or not she was a witch (and there are differing views on this), she serves as a symbol for all those witches and others who have been tortured and murdered for practising their religion and for

possessing psychic powers and charisma. It is important that we remember these people's lives and deaths, even though we know them to have moved onward into other lives and other dimensions, and though they may even be among our own previous incarnations.

Leader: This day we speak
to those who passed through death
by burning, hanging, drowning
in the name of our love.

This day we speak
to those who suffered torture
of body, mind and spirit
in the name of our truth.

This day we speak
to those deprived, impoverished,
enslaved, outlawed and scarred
in the name of our love.

You who now are elsewhere
far, or among us,
You who truly or falsely
bore our name,
You who were destroyed
as grass is destroyed,
spring green in us this day
in more than memory.
And in your names
we comfort and we bless

Leader and   all those that are made to suffer
then all,   for race or creed,
verse by
verse: all those that are made to suffer
              for colour of skin,

all those that are made to suffer
for seeking truth,

all those that are made to suffer
for freedom of spirit,

all those that are made to suffer
for helpless minds,

all those that are made to suffer
for age or childhood.

Leader: This day all these
we comfort and we bless,
and in your names
to those who bring the suffering

Leader and   we send truth, send love
then all,   that, like a sword,
verse by   will cut away all wrong,
verse: make pure the heart,
and clear the understanding.

In your names,
and in Her name,
and through Her power
we bless

and raise our hands in blessing

Blessings be!

A Sabbat: Midsummer Eve, 23-4 June

This day is also known as St John's Eve, being the eve of the feast-day of St John the Baptist (24 June). Throughout Europe it was once a fire festival, and a festival in which the symbol of the wheel, representing the turning of the year at this time of the summer solstice, was used. Midsummer fire festivals are still common in North Africa among the Berbers, and in some parts of the Middle East.

This celebration should take place in the open air. First of all, make a circular clearing in the grass for the fire and protect the uncleared grass with a fence of stones. Then at, or shortly after, sunset light the fire. Once the fire is lit, walk round the house, moving clockwise. If the house has a garden, each celebrant should pick flowers, and twigs should be cut from the trees— nine from nine different trees. If this is not practicable, flowers should be bought or gathered beforehand, and the nine twigs also gathered beforehand. Should it prove necessary to make this celebration indoors, a large earthenware bowl with a lit candle in it should be substituted for the fire and placed in a chalk circle on the floor of the room. Round cheeses should be put in a readily accessible place.

After the circuit of the house and garden (or, if the celebration is being held indoors, when everyone is ready), the celebrants should stand in a circle round the fire. They should then, each in turn, throw a twig into the fire, naming the tree from which it comes, in the following manner:

> One is apple in thanks and blessing.
> Two is pear in thanks and blessing.
> Three is oak in thanks and blessing.

and so forth, until the nine twigs have been given and named. The celebrants should then move slowly round the fire with the following words, said in unison or by the leader and repeated by the other celebrants. While they are being said, all should hold up flowers and look through them at the fire.

> Lord of the Sun
> and Lady of the Moon,
> keep your good wheel turning
> to our fortune.

Now make a second circuit, still looking through the flowers, with the words,

Lord of the Sun
and Lady of the Moon,
bring us the best of summer
and its riches.

Now make a third circuit, looking through the flowers, saying:

Flowers to the flowers, heart;
petals to the petals, source;
life to life and life to life.

When the circuit is completed, throw the flowers into the fire.

Leader: Gather the fruits.

Each celebrant should take a round cheese in his hand

Leader: Through the fire of the sun
all that is is newly born
in strength this middle of the year.
Earth is earth and fire is fire.

The round cheeses should then be thrown hand to hand above the fire or through the flames. When every celebrant has thrown and caught at least one cheese, the ceremony may be completed with everyone saying collectively and individually:

All: Blessed be!

If it is desired, and if it is practicable, the celebrants may then leap through the fire, before settling down to a feast which should include apples or other fruit as well as the cheeses themselves. If the celebration takes place indoors, the leaping through the flames can take the form of simply stepping over the candle. The twigs and flowers that are thrown into the fire in the outdoor version should have been placed carefully in the bowl around the candle. The candle should be left to die out of its own accord, and the contents of the bowl be buried in some appropriate place.

Sunfest 19-20 July

20 July was the feast of the sun, of Helios, and the day was given later to St Elias. The sun not only represents fire, one of the four elements, but is also the great life-giver and seed-wakener, the moon's partner, the masculine God.

Place a ring of white candles with a red one at the centre of the spell table. If the celebration is outdoors, a bonfire will do. The celebrants should wear red clothing or at least wear something red. Gold should also be worn.

Leader: This day we give
to the power of the sun,
the strength, the heat
of life, the spirit's fire,
the king who is
the consort of the queen
who gives the earth its life,
who masters clay,
and call sunpower into us
through her mystery
that we may know the
wealth of teeming earth,
the richness of his riches,
his golden crown.
Sun, give us power
in our souls and bodies.

All: Sun, give us power.

Leader: Sun, give us power
to work well on this earth

All: Sun, give us power.

Leader: Sun, give us power
to rejoice and triumph.

All: Sun, give us power.

Leader: Sun, give us power
to live in strength and courage.

All: Sun, give us power.

Leader: The power is ours.

All: The power is ours.

Leader: And we revere and celebrate the power,
and bless the power we own.
All blessed be!

All: All blessed be!

A Sabbat: Lammas 31 July-1 August

Lammas, 1 August, is a festival traditionally devoted to the celebration of the first corn harvest, and the word 'Lammas' may be a corruption of 'Loaf-Mass' (in Anglo-Saxon *hlaf-mass*). It is also, however, in Celtic tradition the feast of Lugh, the sun god, and therefore called Lughnasadh. It has also been called 'the Gule of August', the Welsh word meaning 'feast'. In Britain 1 August became the traditional August Bank Holiday, the occasion for long-established fairs. It seems once to have been a mourning feast for the dead sun god, who would not rise again until the spring, and a harvest celebration, as well as a fire festival.

This celebration may be carried out in the open air around a bonfire or inside the house standing around a circle marked on the floor, or a circular table. A round earthenware bowl should be placed in the middle of the circle or table, and in the bowl a lit white candle set in earth. The celebrants should each have three or more of the following in their hands: ears of wheat, barley or oats; at a pinch, handfuls of any grain will do. The celebration should be begun by the leader, thus:

Leader: Earth Mother, giver of bread
and of blessings, hear
this our gratitude
for the wealth of the year.

[In turn, moving slowly clockwise round the circle, each celebrant, beginning with the leader, should place one of his offerings in the bowl or in the fire, saying:]

All in   This is a part of all
turn: to thank for all.

Leader: Earth Mother, who are also
the Lord of the Sun,
ripeness and ripener,
loam and swollen grain,
hear our gratitude
for every gift
on this one day of harvest
of many harvests.

[Again, the celebrants should circle, placing their offerings in the bowl or the fire, saying:]

All in   This is a part of all
turn: to thank for all.

Leader: Lady of Gladness,
you have made us glad.
Having been blessed,
we ask the power to bless.

The leader,   With this gift
then all in   give us the power to give.
turn: This is a part of all
                 to thank for all.

[The celebrants and the leader should then cease circling, and the leader should say the following words, each verse being repeated after him by the celebrants.]

Leader,   As the night is the womb of the day
then all: and the day of the night,

> each being in each other,
> so we, together,
>
> man being present in woman,
> and woman in man,
>
> revere and ask a blessing of
> holy earth
>
> on all that is born and dies,
> that dies and is born,
>
> on all that is bound and loosed,
> is loosed and is bound,
>
> on all that rises and falls,
> that falls and rises,
>
> and on ourselves
> that we may love and serve
>
> in joy and gladness now
> in joy and gladness.

Leader: So let it be and blessed be.

All: Blessed be!

The celebrants should then eat and drink together. The meal should include whole-grain bread, malt liquor and anything that involves flour or corn in its making.

If the celebration has been held outdoors, the fire will consume the celebrants' offerings. If it has been held indoors, the candle should be left to go out of its accord, and all the contents of the bowl should be buried in some appropriate place.

Diana's Day (12-13 August)

Diana is the Roman name for the Triple Goddess, who has had various other titles over the centuries. She has been called both 'Lady of Wild Creatures' and 'Queen of Witches'. As Diana Egeria, she was the goddess of healing, and of childbirth. As Diana Nemorensis, she was the goddess of the moon grove. Her three aspects can be summed up as being the goddess of the moon or 'Lunar Maiden', the 'Mother of All Creatures', and the huntress and destroyer. Diana of Ephesus was equated by the Gnostics with Sophia, the grandmother of God. In the fourteenth century a bishop of Meaux stated that 'Diana' was an ancient name for the Holy Trinity. The Romans set aside 13 August as Diana's feast-day, and it is nowadays celebrated by Christians as the feast of the Assumption of the Virgin Mary.

The table or altar should bear three candles, and some wild flowers and herbs. Each celebrant should have a silver-coloured coin, silver being the moon's metal. These are to be given as offerings, and after the ceremony they should be set aside and kept for further ceremonies or for use in some activity appropriate to Wicca.

Leader: This is the day of Diana, Artemis, Isis.
In celebration of her, in her, through her,
in these names and all others,
we light three candles,
Maiden, Mother, Crone,
and ask her blessing
that her power may move in us through us
to love and healing and to wisdom. Thus
we ask health in our bodies to do good.

All: We ask health in our bodies to do good.

Leader: We ask health in our spirits to do good.

All: We ask health in our spirits to do good.

Leader: We ask health in our minds that we have wisdom.

All: We ask health in our minds that we have wisdom
         and in token cast
         these silver coins.

[Each throws a silver coin into the dish, saying:]

All in turn: This is token for love and understanding and
              in praise and thanks.

All: In praise and thanks.

Leader: Blessed be!

All: Blessed be!

Day of Tides (24-25 August)

This day was dedicated in the past to Mari, 'Mother Sea', and as late as 1678 the Irish were worshipping the divinity of Loch Maree, whose island, Inis Maree, contained a temple dedicated to 'St Mourie'. Though her attribute as Mother Sea was emphasized by many, she was also considered a trinity and included the earth and the heavens in her person. Her blue robe represented the sea, and her pearl necklace the sea foam. Another of her names was Moera, which means 'older than time'.

The celebrants should each carry something of the sea, pearls or shells, and ideally, also wear something blue. The table, or altar, should have a sea shell or sea shells on it, and three candles, two blue and one white.

Leader: The tides rise,
        the tides fall,
        advance, withdraw,
        withdraw, advance,
        older than time,

creating time:
this is one name
of the Lady,
and this name
this day we honour.

All: And this name
this day we honour.

Leader, then Life from death
all, verse and death from life,
by verse:

every beginning,
every end,

this name, this day,
we praise.

Leader: Mother of every
wave and tide
through us, round us,
over us, Mother
of every making
every breaking,
every birth and
dance and death,
Mother of all
that lives, yourself
the every life,
this day we praise
the life that is
and is in You,
from you, through you,
we praise and bless.

All: We praise and bless.

Leader,
each line
repeated
by all:

Lady of tides we bless and praise.
Lady of moving dancing waters,
Lady of love we praise and bless.
Lady of giving and of taking,
Lady of life we bless and praise
this day in you.
All blessed be!

A Sabbat: Alban Elfed (20-21 September)

The autumn equinox occurs when the sun moves into Libra.
It is usually celebrated on 21 September. The ancient druid name
for the day is Alban Elfed. 21 September is also the feast-day of St
Matthew, whose symbol in Christian iconography is a man with
wings.

This ceremony should take place indoors. The celebrants
should gather around a circular table or in a circle. In the middle
of the table or circle should be fruits of the harvest— apples,
pears, nuts and other fruits. A bowl of wine should also be placed
there, together with a ladle. Each celebrant should have an empty
wine-glass either on the edge of the circle or on the edge of the
table. Four dishes should be set around the gathered fruits, one
containing a lit candle, one earth, one water and one empty,
symbolizing the four elements. The leader begins:

Leader: In the name of Earth and Air,
        of Water and Fire,
        in the name of the God and the Goddess
        and the wealth of the year,
        here we gather
        in gratitude and blessing.

All: Here we gather in gratitude
        and blessing.

Leader: To receive the gift
        is to bless the giver:
        I give and receive a blessing
        in love and praise.

[The leader takes one item from the store. All the other celebrants, turn by turn, starting on the leader's left, follow suit. When this is done, the leader says:]

Leader: We have been given food
and are given food
We have been given drink
and are given drink
We have been given breath
and are given breath
We have been given light
and are given light
Now in the strength
and power of all these given
we call for the strength
and the power of the season
to bear us on through the year
as the great wheel turns,
to guard us, warm us, bless us
gathered here,
each in the other, together
and at one
in this feast of acceptance,
taking hands

[All link hands and say in unison, moving round the table clockwise:]

All: We are a part of all.
We give and are given.

The circling completed, the hands are loosed and the leader takes up the ladle and gives each celebrant wine, moving round the circle clockwise, ending by filling his or her own cup and raising it and saying:

In the Name of All
and the All that is over All,
blessed be!

All repeat in unison, 'Blessed be!', and drink of the wine.

Eldmas (11-12 October)

This day is given to Edwin, King of Northumbria (584-633). Edwin was a pagan for all but the last six years of his life. His capital was York. The Ogham letter for the month is Eadha (E) and in tree symbolism is the tree of old age or the shieldmaker's tree. This being the last ceremony in this calendar before the new year begins at Samhain, it is proper to devote it to the theme of age.

Each member of the group should wear something that is old and precious, at least to the wearer. Dried autumn leaves should be placed upon the table, and red wine, and three apples, one of which is cut transversely. The ceremony should be held indoors, for this is a ceremony of strength and comfort, and the house is a symbol of these and of security.

Leader: This day we speak
to the old ones
who are here
in every breath we breathe,
in every pulse.

This day we look
into the eyes of age.

This day we stand
beneath the tree of age,
the wide-spread boughs,
the strength of years on years.

This day we look
on this face of the Goddess,
calling into us
her wisdom's power.

Leader, then   Lady, fill our minds
all, verse   with your lasting knowledge.
by verse

                Lady fill our hearts
                with your long-held love.

                Lady grant our spirits
                your ancient cunning.

                That we may move
                through year on year
                in strength,

                that we may learn
                to walk the road of wisdom,

                that we may hold
                compassion for the old
                and reverence for the old
                and bring them joy.

Leader: This day we celebrate
           the wealth of age,
           the riches age
           bears onwards to the gate
           that opens on an elsewhere
           that surpasses
           this time's understanding.

           Lady, here,
           in you, through you,
           we gather strength and wisdom,
           and all old goodness,
           the great spreading tree
           that is both depth and height.

Leader and   We raise our arms
then all: within its branches
               now in power and praise

Leader: and in this power
we bless and we are blessed.

All: We bless and we are blessed.

Leader and   All blessings be!
then all:

Moon Rituals

The sun is celebrated at the high point of summer in a Sunfest, as we have seen. We cannot, however, fit a moon festival to any particular night, and therefore the moon rites may be performed at any time during the year when the celebrants think it proper. The moon is important to Witches, for one of the personalities of the Goddess is that of Selene the Goddess of the moon, and it is the moon which rules the tidal flows of the earth and the body and deeply affects the human psyche. For many witches moon worship is central to their religion, and their magic is performed at a time when the moon is in an appropriate phase.

Ceremony at the New Moon

If the celebration can take place outdoors the celebrants should gaze up at the moon while saying the words, and in the centre of the circle there should be an earthenware bowl of water. If the bowl is so placed that the water reflects the moon, they may concentrate upon the reflection rather than the moon itself, for this represents the moon as a spiritual power; it is in the 'other space' of psychic perception. If the ritual is to take place indoors a paper image of the crescent moon should be floated in a bowl of water at the centre of a round table, or in the middle of a circle on the floor. The bowl, ideally, should be black.

Leader: Mover of tides, of seas, of blood,
and then all   of all the streams of flowing life,
line by   Mother of vision and of birth,
line: through you, in you, this night we draw
                  down to us your light and power.

Leader: This is the beginning. We renew
    ourselves this night, renew our truth,
    our love, our joy, our strength, our knowledge,
    in this time and through this time.

All together: In love and praise we are renewed,
    renewed, renewed, in power and praise,
    here in darkness and in light.

    Blessed Be!

Ceremony at the Full Moon

This differs from the previous ceremony only in having an image of the full moon floating in the water. This may be made of white paper, or it may take the form of a white flower if the reflection of the moon itself cannot be seen.

Leader and   Mover of tides, of seas, of blood,
then all,   of all the streams of flowing life,
line by   Mother of vision and of birth,
line: through you, in you, this night we draw
    down to us your light and power.

Leader: Purified within your mirror,
    rounded and complete of purpose
    in the fullness of your presence
    we accept in love, in joy,
    the strength and wisdom that are yours
    in this time and through all time
    your power our power,
    your peace our peace.

All together: Strong in you, we praise and bless.
    We praise and bless in peace and love.
    Blessed Be!

Ceremony at the Dark of the Moon

The celebrants should wear black, and the bowl of water, whether indoors or outdoors, should contain no symbol. As the words are spoken the celebrants should gaze into the bowl.

Leader and   This is the deep of dark, of birth, of death.
then all, line   This is the deep of powers past our knowing.
by line: This is the well from which the light is drawn
              This is the central growing place of wisdom.

Leader: In this dark we bless the dark of being,
            and learn the strength that centres in the dark
            and brings us from its fullness our beginnings.
            Dark, fulfill us in our hidden selves.

All together : In this night we bless the tide of time
                that moves us through the darkness to the light,
                and call to us the vision that we need.
                In darkness as in light, all blessed be !

                Blessed Be !

Part III

Workbook

Introduction

There are many pagan communities that celebrate the changes of the year with rituals and ceremonies that involve singing, dancing and feasting together. On these occasions they do raise a considerable amount of spiritual power, of energy, but it is often dissipated by there being no single common intent in the gathering. Nevertheless, all present have a triumphant sense of sharing and experience afflatus, perhaps even hubris. Some people believe that the experience of group sharing and of group excitement is the very heart of the religious life. Some believe that the excitement derived from mass emotion and mass imagination is the centre of things. When this is so, the religion may become merely a form of self-indulgence and of collective reassurance. The members of the group become addicted to ceremony and do not perceive that true religion must be central to the whole life of its adherents. One must give, act, work, not merely celebrate, meditate and accept. It is not enough merely to 'raise consciousness', to increase 'awareness' and to 'share'.

Those who have read and sympathized with the rituals in this book may still not feel that acts of magic are necessary to complete the religious experience. The true witch, however, knows that to raise energy and then not to use it in work is wasteful. One cannot, must not, call oneself a witch if one does not use the power in magical work; that is to boil water and cook nothing, to light a lamp and shut one's eyes, to draw the bow and string no arrows.

When it comes to the actual work, the spell-casting part of

Wicca, which is the 'craft' in witchcraft, one must tread a little carefully. The Power, or 'the Odic Force', has been explained in a number of ways. I have come to the conclusion that it operates in three ways, in the main.

First, and most simply, many spells work by auto-suggestion: if a person feels that a spell will work, it will be successful. This is the placebo effect and, even though medical doctors maintain that it is responsible for up to eighty per cent of the cure in many cases, this is regarded by some as not being 'magical' at all. Perhaps it is not, if we only call that which is inexplicable magical. Nevertheless auto-suggestion and hypnosis are ways in which some spells work.

Another way is by means of a kind of telepathy, a message-sending from person to person. The message is sometimes a command, sometimes an encouragement; it directs the subject's mind or body to act or change in a particular way. The message may well be sent by way of a kind of electromagnetic 'wave', 'vibration' or 'pulse', like a radio wave. The message may even be lodged in an object which becomes a transmitter; this is the case with talismans.

A third way is by means of what I can only call 'image transfers'. An image is transmitted, rather than a verbal command. This image-transfer technique involves both symbolism and colour therapy. We are affected emotionally and physically by symbols and by colour.

There are other methods, and most of them are exemplified in this section of the book, but it is hard to provide labels for everything. Moreover, any efficient witch will make use of several methods at once, working, one might say, on different levels or wavelengths at the same time.

The important thing in making a spell is the intensity of the spell-caster's intent. He or she must concentrate a great deal of power into the spell, believing that spells are effective. It is inadvisable, however, to believe too strongly that a particular spell will be totally successful, for then failure destroys one's power to concentrate on later work, weakening it by self-doubt. One must believe that the spell is working, yes, but one can rarely know how completely it will work. Sometimes one is absolutely sure it has worked; one has felt the energy leaving and is filled with happiness and a sense of achievement. Usually however, one knows only that the message has been sent and received, but not if it has been 'understood' by the recipient.

There are many traditions in the Craft, and sorcery is common to many cultures. It is wise to work out the cultural context in which the work must be done. A curse laid upon a person by way of one tradition cannot easily be lifted by someone working in another. An African or Voodoo curse can often be lifted only by a witch working with the symbolism of African or Voodoo magic. Even smaller cultural differences can cause difficulty: Celts can help Celts more easily than they can help Scandinavians; Italians can help Italians much more easily than other folk. We are, it seems, operating in an area affected by what Jung has called 'the racial unconscious'. I am not suggesting that sorcery, or acts of magic, cannot cross racial boundaries; I am only suggesting that, in sending one's 'message', one must take care to choose a 'language' understood by the 'deep mind' of the recipient and that this deep mind has some characteristics gained by inheritance as well as by personal experience and environment.

The spells given here should be regarded more as patterns than as finished products. Every spell-caster must make his or her own spell. Of course, a spell made by someone else may strike one as being entirely sympathetic and totally one's own already. One can enter into it as one enters into a poem and feel the voice of the poem one's own. In those instances there is no need to change the words. In most cases, however, some alteration will be necessary to fit particular problems or particular cultural contexts.

There are omissions here. I have not included that part of the Craft devoted to kinds of divination, for there are already almost countless books on astrology, oneiromancy, cheiromancy, tarot-reading and even casting the runes. Nor have I included any spells to cause harm, for this would be against the Wiccan code and irresponsible.

I should add that almost all the spells included here have been used and found effective. A few of them have not been used exactly in the form printed here but exemplify techniques that have been found successful. A practised witch does not always actually speak the words of a spell; it is sometimes sufficient to think them or to transmit their intent. Some of these spells, therefore, are transcriptions of messages rather than the messages themselves.

One further point must be made. If you use these spells, you are likely to find that at first you are not completely successful. It takes practice to perfect these skills. Also, it is likely that you will find one method easier for you than another. Some witches are gifted with the ability to use their hands effectively as soon as they start; others are not. Some are excellent with verbal magic but weak on talismans. No one is likely to be expert in every field, though with practice one can become a 'general practitioner'. You should never, however, cast a spell simply for practice. There must be real intent within it. If spells are cast without real intent, they often misdirect, and the spell-caster loses any sense of real commitment. That sense of commitment is very important indeed. The craft is no mere game and must not be taken lightly.

Verbal Magic

Love Spells

There are several kinds of love spells. The most successful are those which are made in order to bring an as-yet-unknown lover to the spell-maker. The spell, in fact, appears to send out a general 'radio' message which will be received only by an appropriate person, much as female moths send out a radio message which attracts male moths of the same species. This kind of spell does not attempt to impose the maker's will upon any particular person and therefore does not come up against any real opposition.

1 To Find a Lover

Every Friday night (Friday being the day of Venus, goddess of love), culminating in a Friday on which the moon is full or almost full, throw salt onto the fire from your right hand, saying:

> It is not salt I turn to fire
> but the heart of the man I seek;
> let him have no peace of mind
> until he come to me.

This spell should be cast three times on each occasion. On the third occasion the wording should be slightly altered:

> It is not salt I turn to fire
> but the heart of the man I seek;
> he shall have no peace of mind
> until he come to me.

This concludes the spell. The person sought is unlikely to appear immediately but usually appears within the next few weeks.

This 'seeking spell' can be altered into a 'love-binding' spell by changing the word 'seek' to 'love' or, of course, 'desire', in which case the spell-maker should clearly envisage the person he or she wishes to come. If, however, this particular person resists the 'pull' of the spell, the spell-maker may well find that the force of the spell rebounds and causes extreme anxiety and tension in its originator. This can be avoided by adding at the end of each recitation the words:

> for his good and for my good
> by love's true power.

The word 'man' can of course, be changed to 'woman', and a proper name may be substituted if a specific person is being called. The name should be the personal and not the family name.

2 *To Bring a Lover*

Another 'seeking spell' is one which involves little ritual recitation but does demand a shrewd analysis of the spell-maker's own desires. If you are seeking a partner you may list on one sheet of paper the exact attributes you wish him or her to possess. You might, for example, list kindness, a comfortable income, a love of paintings, and vegetarianism. This list you should then place in a box which has been cleaned with salt, and the box should be left closed and not opened again until the spell has worked. While putting the spell in the box, you must imagine, as intensely as you can, the personality you have described, saying:

> Lady, bring this man to me
> with your power and your love.

You should say this three times and then, after the third repetition, the box now closed: 'So let it be.'

The snag with this spell is simply that it is hard to define a personality completely and that the more complex the description, the longer the spell will take to work. This is a spell for a patient spell-caster.

3   To Attract a Man or Woman

Few people in love are patient. If you desire a person passionately, you can, if you can summon up enough intensity of concentration, bring that person to you in a state of sexual hunger. It would, however, be wise to think at least twice about using this spell. It frequently fails to work because of opposition, but if it does work, the results may be uncomfortably dramatic. There are two versions, one for a woman to attract a man, and one for a man to attract a woman. First, the woman's spell:

> This I lay upon you:
> when we meet
> put your mouth to my mouth,
> and, furthermore,
> this I lay upon you:
> when we meet
> put your breast to my breasts,
> and, furthermore,
> this I lay upon you:
> when we meet
> offer your swelling manhood
> up to me.

The second version runs:

> This I lay upon you:
> when we meet
> put your mouth to my mouth,
> and, furthermore,
> this I lay upon you:

when we meet
put your breasts to my breast,
and, furthermore,
this I lay upon you:
when we meet
open your thighs
and call me into you.

This is a direct 'transmission' from the spell-maker to the person desired.

4   To Command Love

Another spell of the same kind is one derived from the Atharva Veda. It runs:

As the creeper twines the tree,
so your arms will twine round me
in deepest love.

As the eagle rides the wind,
so do I control your mind
to deepest love.

As the sun rules every part,
so do I possess your heart
in deepest love.

This spell makes use of natural symbolism. It does, indeed, bring the forces of nature to bear upon the desired person. In casting the spell, the spell-caster must envisage not only the desired person but also the creeper round the tree, the eagle in the sky, and the sun at its zenith. The same necessity of multiple visualization occurs in the next spell.

5   *To Arouse Desire in a Woman*

Alder of suppleness,
let her lie supple beside me.
Elder, red-lipped,
let her be sweet to my kiss.
Pink-bosomed cherry,
deliver her breasts to my hands.
Fern of the forest,
bare me the clusters of hair.
Smooth-skinned madrona,
slide naked her arms around me.
Whispering wind,
make all her whispers love.
Red-stemmed dogwood,
hurry her veins with fire,
and well, oh, well of the forest,
yield me her depths.

This is a difficult spell to control because it demands so complex a visualization. It may take several hours of practice before you can fill it with the required energy.

It may be objected that this spell has more to do with sexual desire than with love. The majority of love-spells to be found in books of spellcraft are of this kind. It must be pointed out, however, that the spell of sexual desire does not exclude love: the spell-caster can infuse deep affection and true love-yearning into these spells. If he or she does not do this, the magic which is entirely selfish, which is predatory, invariably results in disaster for the spell-maker. That is why it is always as well to work for the good of the person desired as much as for the good of oneself.

The most successful spells of any kind are those which reinforce a desire or feeling that is already present in the person who is the object of magic. This is why healing spells are usually the most effective. No one, unless extremely neurotic, actually wants to be sick. Even if a person enjoys being ill and interesting, there is always somewhere a desire to be well that can be reinforced. The love-spell that is based on the supposition of an already existing sympathy, therefore, is likely to be the most successful. The 'seeking spell' is, obviously, of this kind. So is the following:

6   To Beckon a Lover

> If you are turning towards me,
> know I turn
> also to you
> and come to me in love.
> If you are thinking of me,
> know I think
> also of you
> and come to me in love.
>
> If you are saying my name
> I say your name
> and call you to me:
> come to me in love.

At this point the name should be spoken three times. The literal-minded may think it unlikely that the person addressed will be saying the spell-caster's name at the required time. The word 'saying' has to be taken figuratively, of course, as a kind of shorthand for 'dwelling upon me in your mind'.

In all these cases it is necessary to be able to visualize the person loved or desired. Some spell-makers find that photographs help them do this effectively. One photograph by itself, however, may not be effective, for it shows only one expression, one aspect of the person. A series of different photographs laid out in a pattern on the spell table can, however, be very effective. The pattern should feel appropriate to the spell-caster. In the centre of it a candle may be lit and left to burn out after the spell has been cast. This has the effect of continuing the transmission after the spell-caster has ceased personal transmission. An hour-glass can also be used for the same purpose. These devices are sometimes more effective than the spell-box, which is most useful for long-term magic.

Some spell-casters find it useful also to possess something belonging to the desired one. This may be an article of clothing, such as a glove or scarf. It should be clothing that actually touches the person's skin. An overcoat is unlikely to work unless it is very important to the person involved. Other spell-casters follow ancient practice and secure a nail-clipping or a lock of hair. These are ways to increase the power of the message sent, rather than to assist in mere visualization. They need not be referred to verbally in the spell at all.

7   *Spell with a Love Gift*

Spells are messages. Some love-spells are messages in the form of commands, some, as I have shown, are binding spells, and some are seeking spells. Others, however, do not seek to command the person loved or desired but to work by means of persuasion. The spell does not command the person; an intermediary object or talisman does the work, in the form of a gift which has been energized by the will of the spell-caster. If you wish to affect a loved one by these means, select an object which he or she will wear next to the skin or one that may be drunk or eaten, or that perfumes the air. Perfume and highly scented flowers, especially roses, are traditional love-gifts. Place the gift on your spell-table and say:

> I am within you;
> in your every part
> you hold my name of power,
> my hidden name,
> and speak it to her,
> calling her to me
> in deepest true affection
> and in love.

This should be said three times. The gift should then immediately be wrapped in tissue paper of one colour, not multi-coloured. The colour should be one you feel to be expressive of your affection or your ardour. Red, for ardent passion, would usually be appropriate, but green might also be satisfactory, as being the colour of springtime and of Venus. The gift should then be placed in a box, and the box should be tied up with cord or wool of the same colour as the tissue paper. It should be delivered personally, hand to hand, or (if this is not feasible) by personal messenger, so that it does not suffer from contact with too many other hands or from the energy fields of postal machinery.

8 Binding Spell, using Spell Box

It is not always possible to send a gift. In this situation the spell-caster should take a black polished stone and, having moistened it three times with spittle (do not spit on the stone; moisten it with your finger), say:

> In the name of power
> I give you the name
> X

This should be said three times. Then you should say:

> So let it be,
> and now by my command
> within her live and
> call my name in her
> and bend her will
> to my commanding love.
> So let it be.

The stone should then be placed in a spell box, which should be placed where you can see it clearly and frequently, and beside objects which you feel will reinforce the spell or which are deeply personal to you. Thus each day you will reinforce the spell whenever you see the box.

9 To Break the Bonds of Love

I have already mentioned one danger in making a love-spell, that of its rebounding and causing you the discomfort and anxiety which you have attempted to impose upon another person. A second danger, especially of love-spells of the binding and commanding kind, is quite simply that, if they work successfully, you will find yourself bound in responsibility for the one you yourself have bound. You may, indeed, find yourself in time saddled with a relationship you no longer desire. In your armoury of love-spells, therefore, it is as well to have a loosening spell.

Unfortunately, as in legal marriage, it is often a great deal more difficult to separate than to become joined. Moreover, because the loosening spell is usually made entirely from self-interest, it is liable to fail or to rebound or to bring disaster. It must therefore be made with intense and true compassion, not with resentment or anger. Indeed, you may not have the power to unloose what you have bound, just as those who imposed bans (*geasa*) in ancient Ireland could not lift them without extraordinary and divine assistance. In spellcraft, as in life, one's chickens return to roost.

This time you should work within a circle, for the circle is not only a protection but also a symbol of wholeness, and a means of concentrating power. Begin with an invocation to the Lady:

> Lady of power and of compassion,
> grant me compassion
> and your power
> to loosen, break and burn
> these bonds upon her
> and by releasing bless
> and bless and bless.

This should be said three times or until you feel that the power has been given you. Then envision the person you wish to release and say:

> Flesh to flesh
> the bond is broken.
> You are freed and freely blessed.
>
> Eye to eye
> the bond is broken.
> You are freed and freely blessed.
> Tongue to tongue

the bond is broken.
You are freed and freely blessed

Head to head
the bond is broken.
You are freed and freely blessed.

Heart to heart
the bond is broken.
You are freed and freely blessed.

Loin to loin
the bond is broken.
You are freed and freely blessed.

Breast to breast
the bond is broken.
You are freed and freely blessed.

Name to name
the bond is broken.
You are freed and freely blessed.

At each statement of breaking, envisage a thread between
the two persons breaking; in saying the word 'free', envisage clear
open skies; in saying the word 'freely' visualize light surrounding
the person you are releasing and coming to him or her from all
around. You may also use actual lengths of white thread and
break them in the flame of a candle. When this is over, say:

I give you now
a new beginning
and a happiness.

I give
you ease and comfort,
give your name
into the good hands
of the Lady,
whom I thank,

and thank
and praise
and in whose power
I make this be.

10   A Short Bond-Breaking Spell

The loosening spell above can also be used to separate two other people who wish to be loosed but who cannot contrive it themselves, or, of course, to release one person from an unfortunate entanglement. In this instance the spell should be altered. There may be no need to ask the specific intervention of the Lady. Your own intense concentration, your own magical will, may be enough. If that is so, the spell should begin:

X, hear:
the bond is broken,
eye to eye
the bond is broken...

and so on. It should conclude:

...you ease and
comfort,
bless your ways.
This is my will
and so must be.

This spell should also be made from within a circle. It would also be as well to consider carefully whether or not you are making a spell that runs counter to the will of one of the parties concerned. If this is so, there could be difficulty or trouble unless you are a great deal more powerful than that person. It would, indeed, be wise to do this work together with other people so that the power is increased and the resistance less effective.

Blessings

Blessings, in our present-day society, are often made so perfunctorily that we do not take them seriously. 'Bless you, dear', we say in thanks, or 'Have a good day', as we leave the filling-station. When someone sneezes, we respond with 'Bless you', not even aware of the ancient belief that a sneeze means that the spirit has temporarily left the body and is therefore in danger. Nevertheless, blessings that are made with real intent are true spells and can be extremely effective.

Blessings are of several kinds. One is the general blessing of a person to bring health and happiness; it differs from the healing spell in having no specific intent to cure an ill. Another is the blessing which is intended to counter a general malaise; the blessing of a house after an exorcism has been performed is one of these. The third is a blessing intended to protect a person or place from ill rather than simply to improve the situation; many lullabies may be grouped under this head. The fourth is a blessing upon a particular endeavour to ensure that it is successful; prayers before battle that are part of many religious practices are of this kind.

An example of a general blessing is the following.

1 To Bless in All Ways

Envisage the person you intend to bless, concentrating upon this with closed eyes the better to keep out other images and, speaking rhythmically, feeling each part of the blessing as you pronounce it, say (or think):

> For you,
> through the power of the Lady,
> a helmet of light.
>
> For you,
> through the power of the Lady,
> strength in the mind
> and sweetness and calm and rest
> and strength that is growing

strength to strength
and ease and easeful sleep
and gladness spreading,
thankfulness spreading,
love spreading
through all of your body,
all of yourself,
in the power of the Lady,
by the power of the Lady,
through the power of the Lady.

This spell is directed particularly at improving a person's psychological state, at giving calm and comfort, and could be used as a blessing before sleep, in which case it could be spoken to the person as he or she lies in bed or, if the person would be troubled by so obvious a ritual, just outside the bedroom door.

2   *To Make a Small Plant Grow*

Not all blessings are intended to affect human beings. Indeed, there is a long tradition of blessings for crops and for sheep and cattle and other creatures. This spell should be said while sprinkling the plant with water from your hand.

Small one,
pretty one,
reach up
into the air
I bless
for you.

Small one,
pretty one,
rise, rise,
strong from the
earth I bless
for you.

> Pretty one,
> small one,
> grow big,
> drink deep
> of strength,
> grow tall,
> spread wide
> your leaves,
> bloom strong
> in trust, in love,
> and bless
> this air
> and earth
> and time
> I bless for you.

Obviously this spell can be made to bless more than one plant by changing 'one' into 'ones'. In this case, you should walk among plants, scattering the water as you do so, ensuring that no plant is left unblessed. As with almost all blessings, this too can be given by several people speaking in unison or in turn. It is as well, however, to work out the movements ahead of time, for if everyone concentrates properly on the spell, there may be confusion due to people walking into each other. Unless the plants themselves are laid out in a ring, the usual circle will not be of any help in ordering the group's moves.

3   To Accompany the Gathering of Vegetables

Another spell that relates to the garden is one of thanks. This, like the 'Grace before meat' of the Christian tradition, is no empty gesture, for the blessing alters and improves the quality of that which is blessed.

> I take this
> from the earth
> in praise
> of life and light
> and bless

the good
that comes to me
and thank the good
and this which
gives me
of its worth.

4   *Blessing before Food*

Another blessing which follows logically on from the above
is a 'blessing before food'. This blessing may require some adjust-
ment by vegetarians or for meals which have other limitations.

Earth has given,
Water given,
Air has given,
Fire given
through the power
of the Lady,
in the blessing
of the Lady,
and in her name
and through her body.

We bless this good bread
of her grain,
these the firm roots
of her earth,
these the green leaves
of her sunlight,
this the clear wine
of her vines,
this her gift from
sea and river,
this her gift from
field and forest,
these her fruits
and these her berries,
all, we being blessed,

bless
that this meal be
a feast for her
and through her strengthen
flesh and spirit.

5 Blessing upon a Task

Blessings on particular tasks and projects have always been important. The plough is blessed, as is the first furrow it makes. The first sheaf of corn to be reaped is blessed before the work is permitted to continue. A general blessing that can be used for any task is the following:

Blessing upon the hands,
blessings upon the mind,
blessings upon the skill
in her, through her
this blessing.

6 Blessing on Labour

A more particular blessing, which is in the form of an invocation, may be used to help any artist or craftsman. While this blessing is given in the first person, the word 'my' may be changed to 'his' or 'her' or 'their' as required.

Goddess, bring to these my labours
all for which Your splendour came;
Goddess, bring to these my craftsman
fingers everything You name
as Grace, as Harmony, as Good;
Goddess, bring me all I would
in wisdom wish, in wisdom pray,
and complete this work this day.

7   *Self-blessing for Confidence*

While it is a rule in spellcraft that spells must not be made for selfish reasons, there is no rule against self-blessing or in making spells to bolster self-confidence when facing a particular task or even, simply, the day ahead. The following spell should be said at the beginning of the day and fasting, while envisioning clearly the events, places and people that are to be encountered. If an interview, stage performance, recital or business meeting is ahead, the spell should be repeated silently before the event. It should be recited until there is a strong sense of inward strength and confidence. Three times is the usual number required.

> In this country
> I am the sun;
> life lifts to my gaze,
> my touch, my word;
> the people are held
> in the grasp of my hand,
> the people are bound
> to the sound of my voice;
> the people are rapt
> by the light of my eye;
> this country is mine;
> this day I rule.

If this spell is intended to improve a particular occasion such as a meeting or interview, the word 'day' may be changed to 'hour' which does not, of course, indicate an hour by the clock but a limited period of time.

8   *Invocatory Self-Blessing*

Another invocatory self-blessing has a more general purpose. It is a self-blessing to be spoken aloud or in the mind only at a moment of solitude before a special occasion of difficulty or stress or an important test or encounter. It should be spoken standing, hands raised, eyes closed.

> Since I am alone,
> now come to me,
> becoming me,
> becoming in me, round me,
> becoming how I breathe,
> taste, touch, hear, see,
> becoming how I walk,
> sit, lie down, rise,
> becoming how I think,
> remember, dream,
> envision, prophesy,
> becoming how
> I am alone
> that I may be, alone,
> emptied and filled and whole
> and serve your power.

Spells of this kind are not selfish, in that they include a desire, an intent, to serve and are not egotistical. Few serious spell-makers, however, concern themselves with their own welfare; they are more interested in affecting others.

9   *Blessing for an Infant*

Here is a blessing which may be used to help and strengthen any other person. While it is directed, in this particular text, at the spell-caster's child, the words 'my child' may be changed to 'this man' or 'this girl' or, even more simply, 'this one', without disordering the rhythm. The line 'this my child' may be changed to 'this, this one'. The rhythm of spells is important, for it is the rhythm which gives authority to the words and makes them feel powerful. This particular spell should be chanted.

> Goddess, bless
> my child with strength,
> with all he needs
> of strength and calm;
> Goddess, bless
> my child with good,

O give him good.
Protect from harm
this my child,
defend him, break
all spears that counter him,
uphold
his strength and purpose,
give him good,
and, Goddess, gladness
in his world.

10   Blessing for a Child

A similar and more gentle blessing is the following:

Light, be blessing on my child;
Bring her ease and peace and grace;
Let her burdens fall away;
Let her keep untroubled peace;
Bring her every lovely truth;
Bring her every heart-whole charm;
Bless her in her pride and youth
And protect her from all harm.

11   House Blessing

Whenever you move into a new house or apartment, whether
an old one or one freshly built, it is wise to perform a house
blessing. First of all, decide upon the centre-point of the house. If
the house is on various levels, use one of the landings on the stairs.
Take a cup of red wine and stand at this point and, facing in turn
the four points of the compass, say the following, taking a sip of
wine on each occasion and ending by draining the cup.

Facing east: Lady of Love and Power
and all blessings,
breathe love into this house,
fill air with good.
Through you, in you, I
bless this house.

Facing south: Lady of Love and Living
and all blessings,
warm this house with comfort,
make whole its hearth.
Through you, in you, I
bless this house.

Facing west: Lady of Tide and Time
and every blessing,
let every hour flow sweetly
in this house.
Through you, in you, I
bless this house.

Facing north: Lady of Strength and Riches
and all blessings,
make this house strong
and filled with earthly good.
Through you, in you, I
bless this house.

In conclusion, turning to all four points twice more, repeat:
'You are blessed!'

Banishing

It is sometimes necessary to deal with difficulties caused by imprints of the past left in a house or apartment. The house may feel uncomfortable, may cause the people in it to sleep badly, to feel depressed. This is often the result of neglect. A place made for living must contain living people, and a long-empty house falls sick from a kind of under-nourishment.

1 House-Cleansing Spell

To banish this kind of imprint, one does not need a full-dress exorcism. The house blessing given above may be sufficient. If it is not, walk around the house, into every room, every cupboard, even the attic, if there is one, saying:

Be comforted. All is well.
Now you are blessed.
You have life to nurture
and nurture you.
Be calm. Be easy. Be comforted.
You are blessed.

You will sometimes need to use a hand-blessing, projecting calm and, indeed, happinesses with your lifted hands. You may even, in some rooms, wish to express the happiness you bring with a few dance-steps.

2   To Banish an Unwelcome Entity

More difficult imprints, almost amounting to what we call ghosts, require actual banishing rather than the above, which is really a blessing. If you can identify the cause of the imprint as a particular previous resident, speak directly to him or her in the room which is most affected.

It is time to leave here.
All is well.

There is nothing here for you.
You must be gone.

Go now, Go,
complete your passing.

Go,
and with our blessing
and farewell.

Fare well!

In banishing the imprint, make sure that nothing has been left behind that carries with it a part of the energy field of the previous owner or tenant. Throw out all old pieces of writing in particular, and all photographs.

3   Purification Spell

If there is something you wish to keep that is imprinted with
a previous energy field purify it with salt; if you suspect the furni-
ture, use incense to purify it, saying:

> With this I purify you
> of the past,
> of hurts and memories,
> keeping only love.

There are a number of other banishing methods using a
broom or whisk. Sweeping out a newly acquired house should
also be a sweeping out of all past unhappinesses. The dust should
be swept out of the back door. In this day and age, it is likely that
you will use a vacuum cleaner, of course. Should that be the case,
when you have vacuumed, use a broom symbolically. The point of
this is that you yourself must feel that a real 'clean sweep' has been
made. If you cannot be assured of this, you will feed your unease
and allow it to increase.

A very straightforward way of counteracting a residue of
unhappiness in a house or apartment is, quite simply, to hold a
house-warming. The house is presented with gifts and feels blessed.
At a witch's house-warming at least some of the gifts should be
symbolic.

Healing

There are many kinds of healing magic, and by no means all
make use of words. Verbal magic, is, however, the best place to
begin. First of all it must be emphasized that all healing spells
must, wherever possible, be based upon a sound diagnosis made
by a doctor, for it is often possible to clear up symptoms without
affecting their cause, and thus do harm to the subject. When there
are no symptoms or danger signals, it may be assumed, incor-
rectly, that a cure has taken place, and this may have unfortunate
results.

Secondly, it must be realized that in some cases a person may actually wish to be ill, may feel the illness has been deserved. This person may consciously desire to be healed but subconsciously insist on being ill. This is why Jesus, in healing, began the process by saying, 'Thy sins are forgiven.' It is necessary, sometimes, to begin a healing spell by removing anxiety or guilt. In severe cases a 'bondage-breaking' spell may be necessary. The following spell to ease excessive menstruation includes this element.

1   *To Cure Excessive Menstrual Bleeding*

Lady of Blessings, heal her mind,
cleanse it of all fear and shame,
purify her dream and thought,
cleanse her heart of every stain;
Lady of Blessings, make her strong
to sleep in ease, to wake in joy,
to walk tall in the air she wears;
Lady, heal! Oh, Lady, bless!

Lady of Blessings, bring her peace;
bring calm and strength to all her ways;
cleanse her mind of shame and pain;
still the flowing cunt of blood.

Let the blood be stilled.
Let the blood be stilled.
Let the flow be eased.
Let the blood be stilled.

Lady, Lady, Lady,
through these words
clench the broken flower of blood,
dry the river of the red,
strengthen purity of limb.

Lady, Lady, bring to her
ease and comfort.
Lady, Lady
through these words
her I make whole.

Lady, seal her flow of blood.

2 *To Ease Menstrual Pain*

A simpler and more direct spell for the same disorder is the following. It should be repeated at least three times or until the spell-caster is assured that the spell has worked.

Red flower,
hurt flower,
heal, bless
this lady with
all happiness,
all wealth of mind,
all ease of soul,
that the new day
find her body whole.

This is, obviously, a spell to be made at night or in the evening. It is directed straight at the woman's body.

3 *Invocation to Ease Menstruation*

A third spell is directed to the Goddess.

Lady, let the blossom fail,
let the bloody blossom dry,
bring the peace of love to loin,
bring her ease of heart and mind.
Lady, let the blood be small
and gentle in her woman place,
give her ease, O give her ease
and peace and peace,
O peace, O peace.

In making these spells it is important to give the spoken words intensity, and to allow your body to move and sway, your hands to gesture, even your feet to move in the fashion you feel instinctively matches the words and the spell's intent.

4 *To Assist a Woman to Conceive*

Spellpower is particularly effective in dealing with infertility. The following spell to make a woman conceive should be said three times.

> It is the time of harvest.
> Your womb fills.
> The ears of the grain are swollen.
> Your womb fills.
> The ears of the grain are splitting.
> It is time.
> Bring forth!
> Bring forth!
> Bring forth!
> In the power and the love.

5 *To Cause a Natural Miscarriage*

Sometimes, as above, the spell is a direct action by the spellcaster who has summoned up the psychic power in himself or herself. On other occasions, as in some curses, the power of the spell is made dependent upon the Goddess herself. Here is an example of a spell which includes what might reasonably be described as prayer. It is a spell to cause a miscarriage. It should be used only rarely and for good reasons.

> Take back this gift.
> Let the womb release
> the human fish
> in its bubbled seas.
> Unclench the gut.
> Let the birth run out
> that none may be hurt
> in flesh or heart.

Muse, Powers, Spirits,
Beings of Light
and Fire and Poetry,
grant my thought
your power to act;
I pray that she
may be in all ways
granted mercy.

This spell, like many, may be accompanied with an appropriate action. In this case the breaking of an egg into a dish would intensify the message. The egg should then, of course, be buried in the earth.

6   To Banish Pain

Many spells of healing can be accompanied by actions. The following spell against pain makes use of knots. Knot magic is very old and is used both for healing and for binding. The cord used should be black in this instance.

I lay this cord on the hurt.
The hurt comes into the cord.
I tie a knot in the cord.
It is as I say.

Hurt comes into the cord.
Hurt you are trapped in the cord.
Twice trapped in the cord.
It is as I say.

Hurt comes into the cord.
Hurt you are trapped in the cord.
Thrice trapped in the cord.
It is as I say.

I take away the cord
that holds the imprisoned hurt.
The hurt has come away.
It is as I say.

I bury the cord in the earth.
Earth, receive this cord,
make it earth of earth.
It is as I say.

This spell can be performed on the body of the sufferer or at a distance, the spell-caster visualizing the painful place. It is often better and more efficient to work at a distance with this kind of spell, as the subject may well react to the spell with distrust or scepticism, or even a curiosity and interest that block the transmission of the message.

7   To Bring Sleep

The healing of pain can be achieved in many ways. Some constant or chronic pains are better treated by talismanic magic, and this I will deal with in a separate place (p.184). Sometimes the problem is to get the subject to sleep. Again there are talismanic methods to deal with insomnia. There is also, however, a verbal spell:

Sleep be with her,
clean sleep.
Wings of darkness bring
sleep to her,
clean sleep.
Let her mind be
filled with hushing
waves and winds of
deep sleep,
sleep soothing,
dreams blessing,
heart resting,
mind eased.

8   To Bring Sleep to a Child

Another spell, which is also a prayer, is to give a child a good night's sleep.

Let her sight
be calm, be peace;
let the sealing
darkness come
kindly on her inward gaze
quiet in the quiet room.

Let the sight
of night and dream
be clear, be clean,
be soft, be calm;
Lady, give this child
your ease,
and hold her warm
from any harm.

9   To Ease a Child's Ear-ache

A frequent cause of disturbed sleep in children is ear-ache. Here is a spell that should be spoken under the breath while standing over the child in his or her bed. It should be repeated three times.

To the brow coolth;
To the ear ease;
To the face calm;
To the mind peace.

10   To Ease Ear-ache in General

Let the ear be whole
and the calm seas
live in the movements
of her breath;
let the ear be healed
and the great winds
move softly
in all her moves;
let the ear be healed

let the ear be healed
let the ear be healed
and a good sleep
bring happiness
bring health
bring calm;
let the ear be healed.
So let it be.

11   *To Heal Eye Inflammation*

Eyes be eased.
Eyes be pure.
Eyes be clear
and eyes be sure.
Eyes be whole.
O, eyes be whole,
and eyes be light
unto the soul.

12   *To Cure Defective Vision*

You who have power of vision, bless
these eyes with ease, with colour, light,
with clarity, and calm, and peace
that make them paths through every night
and every day, surefooted tracks
for this hurt woman; give her ease
and light of sky and sun and cloud
and grass and green and seas and trees
and every sharp delighting thing;
ease every pain; ease every stress;
view through her eyes and in her eyes
the utter health of holiness.

13   *Short Spell to Heal Eyes*

The shorter the spell, the easier it is to give it full intensity. The following spell for eye disorder should be chanted:

>Heal
>Heal
>Balm
>Balm
>Eyes
>Heal
>Soul
>Be calm

14   *To Cure Soreness of the Throat*

Ideally this spell should be accompanied by hand movements, the hands, in vision, stroking the throat of the subject.

>Let the throat be pure
>Let the voice be strong
>Let the Healing Light
>the Healing Warmth
>the Healing Ghost
>transform and bless
>the Voice   the Voice   the Voice   the Voice.

This spell is a direct command. Such spells can always be completed by saying 'It is done and blessed be', or 'So I will; so must it be.'

There are countless recipes to cure warts and skin disorders. Here are two. In casting these spells one must envision the cleanness and smoothness of skin.

15   To Cure Skin Disorders of the Hand

Lady, let the hands be clean.
Let a smoothness grace the skin.
Let the nails be strong and firm.
Let the hands be young and warm.
Give good grace, O give good grace.
Bring this lady peace and peace.

16   To Cure Skin Disorders

Let the skin be smooth
upon the hand.
Let the skin be sleek
and smooth and pure.
Let the wholeness come
upon the hand,
and purity and grace
and grace.

17   To Banish Warts

There are many dwindling spells to deal with warts. Some of these are grotesque, and I will not mention them here. Knot magic is often effective. A knot should be tied in a cord (black) for each wart, and the knotted cord thrown into the fire. Words may not be needed, but if words assist the spell-caster's concentration, he or she might recite:

The wart is come in the knot;
The wart is trapped in the knot.

The wart and the knot are gone.
The wart and the knot are gone.

18   To Ease Aching Bones

Simple pain is often difficult to deal with, for pain, especially constant pain, perpetuates itself by a process of anticipation. We expect to feel the pain; therefore we beckon it to us. A straightforward spell for aching bones is the following:

> Lady, heal her bones of pain.
> Lady, ease her bones of hurt.
> Bring her cleanness of all bone.
> Bring her strength in every part.
> Lady, heal, make whole each limb.
> Lady, bless, oh bless, oh bless
> and strengthen, ease and comfort.
> Lady,
> give this one of yours your peace.

19   To Ease Arthritis

> Straightness of tree
> make this limb firm.
> Smoothness of stone
> make this joint strong.
> Power of tide
> make this hinge clean
> that the body stand straight
> and the heart be well.

Most healing spells should be made in terms of the particular subject and used for that subject only. The above spells are simply examples of the way spells can be made. Sometimes it is necessary to include, within the spell, a command to the person to do the necessary work himself or herself, as in the following spell:

20   To Cure Stomach Disorders

> Let the soft belly become warm
> with firm comfort, the bowel move
> in certainty, the heart unharmed,
> the body heal itself with love.

Goddess, be the bearer of
this message to him: Heal! Heal!
Cure thyself and cure thyself.

Goddess, give him now the real
and inward knowledge; let him have
the understanding of his way
and of his need and so be healed.

Goddess, bring him every day
all peace and ease and strength that is,
and make this message in his blood:
Heal! Heal! Goddess, give
this man all that there is of good.

This combines both healing and blessing. It is good to do
this, specially when the illness has become so significant to the
sufferer as to constitute an important part of his life-attitude.

21   To Cure Irregularity of the Heart

Heart, Heart, beat steady,
steady beat, steady beat,
steady, steady, steady, steady.
Blood run easy, easy, easy,
steady, steady, steady, steady, steady.
Heart beat steady, steady,
Blood run smooth
and Pulse be steady, steady, steady.
Heart be steady,
Heart be whole.

This should be chanted, and the spell-caster should add to
the message with body movement.

It is important to use the body in making spells. Spells to ease
breathing involve the spell-caster in breathing deeply and regularly, even loudly, as if he or she is breathing for the sufferer.
Indeed, the spell-caster may add his or her own will to that of the
sufferer. This feeling oneself into the subject can sometimes be a

little dangerous, for one may take on some of the symptoms oneself after the spell is done.

22   *To Heal a Tree*

To end this section, here is a spell, which must also be deeply felt, to heal the dying branch of a tree. It can, of course, be used to heal plants other than trees.

> Sap rise,
> rise rise
> into this
> bough
>
> bring sprig
> bring leaf
> sap rise
> rise rise
>
> sap run
> run run
> along this
> bough
>
> bring power
> power
> and heal
>
> sap sing
> sing sing
> within this
> bough
> sing sing
> sing sing
> in this bough
>
> and in this
> tree that now
> is whole

and healed
and singing.
Blessed be!

Bidding and Binding

There is some danger in using bidding and binding spells frequently, for the spell-caster may become attached to the sense of power which the successful use of these spells brings with it. Curses (which are, of course, essentially bidding and binding spells) are particularly dangerous, because if they meet with opposition they can rebound upon the spell-caster. The only safe kind of curse is a conditional one, which cannot rebound because the stated conditions do not apply to the spell-caster.

Because the law of Craft is 'Love and harm no one', all banishing spells and curses should, perhaps paradoxically, include a blessing element. No spell should be made that is not ultimately life-enhancing

1   *Banishing Spell*

If this one
has hurt this other one,
let him be racked
with the same pain.

If this one
has cheated, lied,
let him be cheated
and be slandered.

If this one
has made this place
uncomfortable
for this other,
let him now
depart this place
in health and whole,
but not return.

2   Banishing Invocation

Lady, have mercy on this woman.
May he that afflicts her go away,
not in sickness or in sadness
but in health and ease and peace.

In making spells that are likely to be opposed, either by the will or by the subconscious of the subject, one must protect oneself. One can do this in several ways. One obvious way is to work within a protective circle; another is to wear a protective talisman until the spell has worked.

Binding spells require enormous energy and should, ideally, be followed immediately by a precise series of commands to the person who has been bound to the spell-caster's will. Binding spells should involve actions as well as words. The following spell should be cast while winding thread around a twig, as on a spool. The twig should be lettered with the subject's initial or name. Of course, a photograph of the subject can also be used, and some spell-casters would also attach a strand of the subject's hair or a nail-paring, or something which has been in close contact with the subject, such as a handkerchief, or a fragment of one. The completed object should be placed in a small box, and left there. When the time comes for the spell to be removed, the spool can be unwound. To bury the twig in the earth or burn it would make it much more difficult to undo the spell. One should say in passing that it is always harder to remove a spell than to cast one.

3   Binding Spell

Wound and bound
wound and bound
so the words of will
resound,
holding, binding,
clasping firm
this man, this man [this chosen woman]
that now is mine
to bid and bind

to bid and bind
deeply deeply
with my mind.

The colour of thread used (silk is particularly effective) and the kind of twig should be appropriate to the command that is to follow the binding. This binding spell can obviously be used as a preliminary to healing.

4   Silencing Spell

Sometimes a specific binding spell is needed. Here is one to silence a wicked tongue.

Lady, I pray you,
still this man.
May his tongue lock,
his lips be shut,
till silence bring him
love and truth
and there is glory
in his heart.

5   To Cure Obsession

Quite frequently one comes across situations in which a person, or persons, appears to have been already bound, already imprisoned or trapped. It may be that a person is obsessed with something or some person. It may be that this is causing him or her suffering. In such cases a spell for breaking bondage is needed.

At each verse of the following spell a black thread should be broken, either in the hands or by holding it across a candle flame and pulling. At the conclusion the threads should be burned up in the candle flame or thrown into the fire.

Lady, unloose
what binds and holds
this one to that
which is not good.

Lady, release her
of those bonds
that harm her and
prevent her ways.

Lady, break
the fetters clasped
upon this one
that she may be
freed to herself
and to your love
and to all good
and truth and mercy.

6 Short Spell to Cure Obsession

As with all these spells, the spell-caster must make adjustments for particular cases. A simpler way of releasing bondage is to place a photograph of the subject before you and break the threads in the candle flame over and over again, saying:

This is a bond and it is broken.
Of this bondage you are free.
By the power of the Lady,
as I will so must it be.

7 Binding Spell with Photograph

Sometimes the binding can be done almost entirely by the power of one's intent. Take the photograph of the subject, or visualize him or her clearly, and say over and over again:

I speak to you and bid you hear.
I speak to you and bid you hear.

When you sense that communication has been achieved, you may continue with: 'These are my words and this my will' or with whatever message or command you wish to deliver.

If spell boxes are used in the casting of these spells, once the spell's purpose has been achieved, the spellbox should be cleansed by filling it with rock salt or sea salt for twenty-four to forty-eight hours. If this is not done, the box may retain some of the energy you have placed within it and confuse later spells.

Talismanic Magic

There are almost countless traditional talismans which can be bought in shops, and they can be used provided they are first cleansed in salt for forty-eight hours and then imbued with energy and with intent. The intent must not run counter to the talisman's traditional significance, however.

One kind of talisman is worn on the person. For a talisman to be effective magically, it should be concealed. Openly worn talismans may signal your attitudes, beliefs and wishes to other people, but they are only 'identity' talismans, and their effect is limited. These are the badges, the old school ties, the labels of the talisman tradition. Talismans concealed on the person retain their power longer: they are not subject to the curiosity, interest and hence energy fields of others.

The most effective talismans are those that are specially made by the spell-caster for a precise purpose. The simplest one is a protection talisman to be worn around the neck.

1 Protective Talisman

A piece of polished metal which is convex on one side and concave on the other is an effective protection device. The mirrored sides return any hurtful vibrations, reflect them back. These pieces of metal can be found as parts of many fishing lures, and, of course a spoon, or the bowl of one, will do nicely. The talisman should be empowered by concentrating upon it, allowing it completely to fill one's field of vision and directing it to protect, giving it an energy field and concentrating power into it. It may be worn on a silver-coloured metal chain or on a thong or cord, whichever is available.

Talismans of this kind can be made in batches and then placed in a spell box for safe-keeping. They should ideally be wrapped in a piece of silk, and the box should be wooden or ceramic.

2   Sleep Stones

Talismans are unlike purely verbal spells in that they continue to send out their messages, rather like radio transmitters, whereas the verbal spell ends when the spell is cast. The talisman is given the message to send, as in the following spell to cure insomnia.

Place polished white or near-white pebbles in a silver bowl, on a silver tray or on the glass of a silver-backed mirror. Place four sticks of incense round them and light the incense. Also light a white altar candle, or all the candles in a three-branched candlestick, if you prefer. Say to the pebbles:

> Sleep is in you
> sleep moves through you
> sleep surrounds you
> carry sleep
>
> carry calm and ease and peace
> carry calm and ease of mind
> carry quiet to the body
> carry quiet to the heart
>
> sleep is in you
> sleep moves through you.
>
> In you now
> I place this sleep,
> the sleep of healing
> dreams and quiet,

the sleep that comforts,
eases, calms,
the sleep that is the soul's
refreshment;
bear sleep thus
to one who holds you,
bear sleep to the one
that keeps you
under pillow
asking sleep;
give sleep in answer:

this I work now
through her power,
this command;
as I command
so must it be
and blessed be!

The pebbles should be placed in a box of their own, together with one or two small feathers, or wrapped in silk. When one is to be used, it should be placed in a little bag of silk with a drawstring and kept under the pillow of the subject. When wakefulness occurs, the sleepstone should be taken from the bag and held in the hand. In the morning it should be replaced in its bag.

This talisman shows the pattern for all talismans. If the talisman is correctly chosen and correctly imbued with its message, it will work. The choice of the talismanic object is crucial. If you are attempting to heal or ameliorate a blood or heart condition, a red polished stone or piece of glass or even plastic might be used. If you are attempting to help hearing, a small conch might be thought appropriate.

3   *Key Talisman to Find Employment*

The key symbol can be a most potent talisman and should be used whenever a 'door' is to be 'unlocked'. One use of the key talisman is to find a person employment. To do this, take a small metal key of the traditional key shape and place it before you on your spell table – or any table you wish, of course – and either write the name of the person you wish to get a job on a piece of paper placed beneath it or simply concentrate upon the image of that person in your mind. Then recite:

> Key, key,
> you are the power
> through the Lady
> and of the Lady,
> here in me,
> and here I say:
>
> Give this man/woman
> [insert name]
> the employment
> he/she desires.
> Open the door
> of good for him/her.
> Open the door
> of his/her desire.
> Open the door.
> Let it be open,
> let him/her enter
> on that work
> which satisfies
> his/her need and will
> and fulfil and
> bless his/her days.
>
> This is your message;
> this your aim;
> this your power
> which now begins.

You may light a white candle and leave the key before it until the candle burns out. This reinforces the message. If the key is laid upon a mirror during the process, this will also help.

The key should be worn by the subject as a pendant, either on a thong or on a silver-coloured chain, underneath the clothing.

Like all talismans that are essentially involved in seeking something, it is unlikely to work immediately. In my experience it will take from three to five weeks, but only if the person himself or herself is also consciously seeking employment. It will not work at all if the person does not think about getting employment and make some effort to get it.

4   Key Talisman to Find Housing

This key talisman can also be used for finding a place to live. If only one person is looking, only one key is needed. If it is a person with two children, three keys might be used, though this is not essential.

The key should be placed as before, and the same kind of formula followed. After the preamble, as in the words for Talisman 3, the spell might run:

> Give this man/woman
> the dwelling place
> of his/her desire—
> a place of blessing,
> comfort, ease
> and safety, warm
> with human good,
> and make this place
> in all ways home
> to all his/her needs.

The last four lines may be as before.

The formulae I have given for verbal spells may, of course, be used also in making talismans; there is no need to repeat them here. The important thing is to ensure that the talisman is in touch with the subject at all times. Thus pendants and rings are particularly effective— especially rings, for these can be worn all night without discomfort, whereas pendants can become twisted and troublesome. Moreover, rings do not usually excite too much curiosity, unless they are bizarre. In selecting rings, always choose those that have a stone of an appropriate colour. If you can afford it, you may use stones that are traditionally associated with particular qualities. There are many books that deal with the supposed properties of semi-precious and precious stones. Here I will mention only a few stones which I know to be magically effective.

5 *Jade Talisman for Relieving Stress*

For reducing tension and anxiety, and ameliorating their physical effects, use green jade, in either a ring or pendant. Small polished pieces of green jade can be bought for very little; green jade rings are even easier to find. The words should follow the formula:

> Peace, Peace,
> Comfort, ease;
> Peace, Peace,
> Comfort, ease.
> The mind easy,
> the body calm.

This should be said several times until it is felt that the message has been placed firmly in the stone. There is no need to give this talisman a particular name, for, like a sleepstone, it will work for anyone to whom it is given.

Green jade is often carved into different shapes, and some of these are appropriate to the jade's function as a bringer of ease. The fish symbol is one of these, for the notion of easy, flowing movement is there, and the fish is also associated with longevity and with natural fertility of spirit.

6 *Amethyst Talisman for Clarity of Thought*

An amethyst has many traditional properties. Basically, however, it brings clarity of mind and strength of imagination. List these qualities while consecrating it. It may also be used, quite simply, to bring good fortune.

7   *Turquoise Talisman to Bring Good Fortune*

Turquoise is helpful in bringing good fortune and success. It also is said to improve people's strength of mind and courage. It is a useful amulet to give to people who are facing difficult situations.

8   *Red Talisman to Bring Vitality*

Any deep red stone – garnet, ruby, carnelian – can be used to help those with weakening disorders, especially of the heart, blood or lungs. It can be used as either a pendant or a ring. A ring is preferable, as then the talisman is constantiy pressed upon a vein. Moreover, the wearer is conscious of it and can touch it from time to time.

The whole notion of touching and caressing rings is interesting. As one touches or strokes a talismanic ring, its message is reinforced. This is, after all, one reason for 'telling beads' in various cultures: as one passes from one bead to another, the message is repeated.

Some talismans may consist of written words— on parchment preferably, though paper will do; some may be made of engraved metal. Wherever possible, they should be made at an appropriate phase of the moon. If the talisman is to strengthen, it should be made while the moon is waxing; if it is intended to make some disorder or pain go away, it should be made when the moon is just past the full.

The shape and nature of the object are important in that it is difficult for a spell-caster to give the message full power if the object does not seem appropriate— it is difficult, but not impossible.

Some talismans should be worn on the body and on the afflicted area. Silver earrings will help with ear disorders, for example, and if a talisman made of a small crystal or crystal-seeming object (a button, for example) is placed in the navel (taped there), it can send its energy all around the stomach, intestines and genitals. If the talisman is intended to have a soothing effect, a smooth blue bead or marble may be used.

Bracelets can, obviously, be used to help hurt arms. There is, indeed, no object that cannot be used.

All these are healing talismans. There are, however, others which are not intended to heal people but to affect a dwelling-place. A talisman at the threshold of a house can be extremely effective.

Much has been written about those Voodoo curses that take the form of a collection of talismanic objects buried under the threshold of the house of the person to be afflicted. Threshold magic can be very powerful and sometimes extremely useful. If a householder is suffering from unwanted visitors, from nuisances, or worse, a threshold talisman can be used to keep people away. There are many of these listed in folk-lore; they range from horseshoes to stones with holes in them (hag stones) and twigs of trees, such as the rowan or mountain ash. When a threshold has been used over and over again unpleasantly, it develops a certain 'vibration' that attracts unpleasantness. The threshold should therefore be cleansed; a sprinkling of salt over the step or under the mat or on the porch steps will clean it nicely. This will keep away nobody of goodwill but will cease to attract ill-wishers. A protection talisman could also be placed under the mat.

Frequently it is important that the subject should not know exactly of what a talisman consists. This is because his or her conscious mind may reject it as being absurd or trivial. What heart patient would believe that a red glass button could be of any value, for example? Talismans of this kind should be sealed within a small box – a pill box or ring box would do – with sealing wax of the appropriate colour or tied within a small bag of coloured silk. They can then be used as pillow talismans or carried in a purse or pocket.

The faith of the subject is always a help; scepticism is always a hindrance. One must do one's best, therefore, to increase the one and defeat the other. In order to do this, some witches overstep the mark and behave as have some priests of other religions, creating by legerdemain or by stage illusion some 'miracle' or other. To give a person a strong belief may be one of the most effective forms of magic known. Unfortunately, however, the tricks of the weeping statue, the ectoplasmic appearance, the fake apparition and so forth are eventually discovered to be tricks, and this means that the witch or priest concerned falls into disrepute and is faced thereafter with a scepticism it is difficult to defeat.

Certainly, in talismanic magic, the acceptance of the talisman by the subject is very important. It is not essential, however. If a person accepts a gift for what it is, without dreaming of its having any talismanic intent, that talisman can still be efficient. Some of these secret talismans are easy to plan and are, indeed, traditional. A woman will happily accept a scarf or a pair of gloves from an admirer. A wrist watch may be given, whose band is a bracelet talisman. So much is obvious. Anything worn can be given talismanic power. One of the most effective is a shirt or blouse for it touches the body at many points. The talismanic shirt was used by the Indian Shaman Wovoka, who gave 'ghost shirts' to his followers, informing them that they would make them impervious to white men's bullets. A war resulted, and the talismans did not work, for all the faith of their wearers. Nevertheless, here is a suggestion for a garment talisman:

9   Garment Talisman for Protection

This armours and protects
through the power
with the power.
This holds healing in its folds
through the power
in the power.
This is the robe of ease and comfort
through the power
in the power.
This in the name of the strength
of the Lady.
So this is.
So it must be.

This should be said three times, and the garment should be passed through a previously energized large ring (silver coloured) or a necklace made of sea shells, preferably cowries.

10   *Talisman to Cure Nose Bleeds*

To cure a nose-bleed, tie a piece of red thread around the left wrist of the sufferer. This is, of course, for nosebleeds that occur spontaneously, not as a result of violence.

Projective Eye and Hand Magic

I have invented the term 'projective magic' to describe a particular use of visualization technique. In many spells one visualizes the change one wishes to make. One certainly visualizes the person one wishes to affect. Projective magic differs in projecting a symbolic image upon that person.

Projective techniques can, and should, be used to augment other spells. In the first three spells I give the image is projected by the third eye; in the fourth and fifth the image is projected by the hand.

1   To Ease Bronchial Disorders

To ease or cure bronchitis or chest disorders, take the two hands of the sufferer in your own and stand facing him. Breathe deeply and summon up the energy. Tell him to close his eyes, and then yourself imagine a bright golden lion-faced sun disc, rays all sharply pointed, in the middle of the chest. Hold this vision as long as you can. It may blur or fade and require a further 'boost'. You will feel the energy leaving you and will know when you have done all you are able.

This is the basic projective technique. Others for common disorders are:

2 To Ease Soreness of the Throat

To ease a sore throat, project a wreath of small ivy leaves around the throat; it draws the inflammation into itself, just as ivy feeds upon a tree.

3 To Ease Inflammation

To ease inflammation of any kind, simply project a cooling whiteness, a bright white light.

4 Hand Magic to Heal Cramps

Summon up the energy through the body into the right hand and then project the image or energy from your open palm. This has the advantage that it can be done at a small distance. No hand-holding is necessary. If one is at dinner, for example, it can be done under the table without anyone noticing if one is aiming at something below the waist. If cramps occur above the waist, it is not dificult to make the correct gesture without it appearing strange. To cure stomach cramps, for example, project healing heat. No exact image is required. The same thing applies to tensed muscles or cramps of any kind.

5 To Bring Comfort to a Room

To make a room more comfortable and cheerful, hand projection can be used to project light upon all the walls or project a specific symbol that brings comfort or happiness. It will affect the room very quickly. One must, however, be careful in choosing one's symbolic imagery. People with powerful energy fields find projection becoming telekinesis, so that the energy turns itself into fact. (It is not wise, for example, to project a row of lit candles upon a curtain). It is unfortunately true that one cannot always estimate how powerful one's energy beam is going to be.

Hand projection is one aspect of hand magic, of course, and that must be described next.

The power of the human touch has long been recognized, and manual manipulation of the body has been thoroughly investigated and used to great effect in massage and acupressure, on which there are many books available. I am not concerned with these. Hand magic is a little different in that no physical pressure or force is involved. Indeed, hand magic requires no physical contact.

6   To Ease Pain of All Kinds

To ease pain, place your hand over the affected part but about an inch away and project a healing beam, at first very gently, moving the hand as if it were a metal-detector seeking something lost. After a while you will sense the centre of the discomfort and can then 'massage' the aura at that point, sending stronger beams of energy. Often you will find it useful to move the hand slightly farther away, to deliver a very strong beam at a particular spot. You are sending an energy beam to affect the energy field.

7   To Heal Sinus Infection

Sometimes both hands should be used. In sinus trouble you may need both hands, one for each side of the face. The two hands may be placed on either side of an affected area and the energy beam sent from one hand to the other. This has been called 'using polarity'. It is very efficient in dealing with tension headaches. Place one hand just over the forehead and the other just a little way from the base of the skull, and send the energy between the hands. As before, you may move the hands a little until you feel they are properly in balance.

Basically you are using your life-force or body energy, which has been labelled differently by many different cultures and peoples, from Paracelsus to Wilhelm Reich, from Ancient Greece to Ancient China. While the hand is the most practical vehicle for projecting this energy, there is no reason why it cannot be projected by other high-energy points of the body.

8   To Lessen Tension

Tension is one of the chronic disorders of our time, and there is a variation on body-magic which always appears to be effective. You must take a long wing feather of an eagle, (if an eagle feather is not obtainable, a long wing feather from an owl or hawk can be used) and brush down the body of the tense person from top to toe, all the way round, as if you were sweeping invisible material down to the earth but not allowing the feather actually to touch the body. After each stroke of the wing feather, shake it three times briskly, as if you were shaking off water-drops. You are in fact shaking off static electricity, for the composition of the large wings of predators picks up static in this fashion. The advantage of this method is that you can actually do it to yourself, though the back presents problems, as it does when you try to scrub it.

Perhaps this should not be called magic at all, any more than the following method of curing certain kinds of migraine.

9   To Ease Migraines

It has been shown that migraines often attack people at the full of the moon. If this appears to be the case, make the sufferer sleep with a patch over the third eye (pineal gland). This simple trick blocks out the moon's transmissions just enough to prevent the migraine. Indeed, this trick can be used to protect anyone who suffers any form of disturbance when the moon is full or almost full. It can also be used as a way of giving ease to those who are hypersensitive to transmissions from other energy fields, for the third eye (pineal gland) is the most sensitive of all the receivers we carry in our bodies.

In projection work it is important to think hard about the colour elements of the image you are projecting. Colour therapy is gradually becoming an important part of holistic medicine. Linda Clark's book *The Ancient Art of Color Therapy* (Devin-Adair, 1982) gives a useful survey. In it she provides a list of the colours which stimulate the secretions of particular glands: Red: liver; orange: thyroid and mammary; yellow: choroid; lemon: pancreas and thymus; green: pituitary; blue: pineal; indigo: parathyroid;

violet: spleen; magenta: suprarenals and prostate; scarlet: testicles and ovaries. Whether or not this is a reliable list, it is safe to say that in projection magic certain colours do appear to be especially effective.

10 Colour Spell for Pain

To soothe and calm a person and decrease pain, project a powder blue. Imagining oneself wrapped in a powder-blue cloak when one lies down to sleep will always help one relax and lose tension.

11 Colour Spell for Anxiety

Green is the colour to use in general healing, and it should be grass-green, neither too dark nor too sharp. It also reduces anxieties and tendencies to inflammation and is a colour of renewal or rebirth, which is one of the reasons why women witches sometimes wear green cloaks.

12 Colour Spell to Increase Vitality

Scarlet is the colour of vitality and, when projected, increases the strength of the blood and the blood flow. It can increase nervous tension as it increases energy, however. It is a great reviver.

All this is predicated upon the notion that colours affect everyone in similar ways, and this is not a wholly wise assumption. The use of red, green and blue, however, does appear to be universally effective. The colours given by such writers on colour therapy as Linda Clark may be effective when used as rays of actual light but may not be as effective in projective magic. More information is needed in this area.

Sympathetic Magic

In the past it was believed that, if something in nature looked like a part of a person's body, it would be able to heal that part. Thus lungwort, because it looked like a lung, was considered good for chest ailments. Oysters were thought aphrodisiac because they resembled a woman's genitalia. Rhinoceros horns appear phallic and are still in great demand to cure male impotence.

We may dismiss this as nonsense, but there is a truth buried within the superstition, as is so often the case. In recent experiments it has been shown that, if two cultures in separate vacuum-sealed glass containers are placed near each other, one culture can affect the other, although there is no physical contact between them. Indeed, it seems that the energy field can pass through physical barriers and transmit a pattern of behaviour if the 'donor' resembles the 'recipient'.

This is one explanation of the efficiency of using dolls, replicas of people, for magical purposes: an exact replica of a subject can be used to affect the subject. It also explains why many cultures think photographs of people 'steal away' the soul of the person portrayed. It is not that they actually steal away the soul but that they make a person vulnerable. This belief in the danger of permitting accurate images of people to be created has caused many taboos. In Mohammedan tradition representational art is forbidden. In some Western societies it was the custom to paint people in roles to which they aspired, thus magically endowing them with those roles. Thus a man might be given the classical draperies of a Greek god, or a woman presented as a goddess. There are innumerable portraits of people in what we would nowadays call fancy dress. These are magical portraits and were either consciously or subconsciously made as such. Even nowadays you will hear a note of slight relief when someone, looking at a portrait, says, 'It doesn't really look like me' or 'It isn't quite me', and it is clear that some of those who buy portraits of themselves do so less out of self-admiration than from self-protection.

With all this in mind, it becomes possible to approach sympathetic magic a little more clearly and to realize that it differs, essentially, from that magic which relies upon visualization of a person. The doll, the photograph, the drawing is, for the purposes of the spell-caster, and the duration of the spell, the actual subject.

1   Using Photographs

Take a black-and-white photograph of the person you wish to help or heal. You may, in certain circumstances, prefer to take the photograph yourself and pose the subject in such a way as to give you something to work on. Thus, if you are trying to heal a person's legs or back, you would ensure that the legs and back were clearly seen. When you have the photograph, colour it appropriately. Thus, if you wish to reduce tension, you could colour a hat or a head pale blue; if you wish to strengthen, you would use red, the colour of vitality, and so forth. While making the alterations, you must concentrate upon the person so that you feel you are influencing him or her directly, not simply turning the picture into the expression of a wish. Words are not necessary, but it is as well to focus your intent by having words to repeat inside your head, such as:

> Strength to the limbs,
> Strength to the hands,
> Strength to the legs etc.

You should take a deep breath between strokes of the paint-brush and make every touch a power-touch.

2 Using Drawings

The drawings of children often reveal a magical intent, although the intent is intuitive, not conscious. Thus the unhappy child will draw images of unhappiness in order to control them. Exhibitions of child art from Guatemala have revealed this over and over again. The pictures look like reportage, but they are more than that. Therefore, if you are tackling a difficult situation, you can make a drawing of it, either in symbols or in a more representational manner. If, for example, you are concentrating upon a person trapped in some way, you may draw the person and then pencil a cage around him or her. You might say to yourself as you do so:

> This is the prison,
> this is the cage,

and so forth. Once this is done, you should then erase the bars one by one, thinking,

> This bar is vanished.
> You are freed

until complete freedom is achieved.

3 Using Dolls (Poppets)

The making of dolls to represent a person or a deity is age-old, and in many cultures the doll, image or idol is presented with gifts in an act of worship or is the recipient of prayers. There is no harm in this as long as it is understood that the image is simply a means of communication, that it becomes the person or spiritual entity only because it is a link and only for the duration of the ceremony.

There are many tales of witches making 'poppets' and causing illness, or even death, by sticking pins or thorns into them. In these days we are familiar with the practice of acupuncture and can understand that the sticking of pins may well have been a healing technique. If you wish to use poppets in healing, you may, indeed, rely on an acupuncture chart to tell you where to stick your pins. On the other hand, you may treat the pins as if they are radium needles and place them according to the actual seat of the pain. The radium needle is, indeed, an excellent comparison, if we believe that the Odic Force is a kind of energy-transmission.

Poppets may be made in several ways. A skilled person may make an actual model in wax, plasticine or clay. Someone less skilled may buy a doll and give it something to wear which belongs to the subject of the spell. If you do this, you should first 'clean' the doll by burying it in salt or washing it in water which you have blessed, in order to 'ground' its existing energies. You may also use the naming ritual to give it the name of your subject. Then you may use verbal magic on it as if it were the actual person, as well as manipulate the 'body', or prick it, in whatever fashion you consider most effective.

When the spell is completed, if you are dealing with a chronic condition, place the poppet in a spell box. If this is not the case, you should clean the doll of the spell by washing it or with salt. If you have named the poppet, you must take away the name as you wash it, saying:

> The spell is done.
> I take away your name.
>
> I take away your name
> by the powers of water,
> washing away each letter
> of your name,
> that your name may once more
> be wholly his/hers;
> this I do in love
> and the power of the Lady.
>
> *Nemo. Nemo. Nemo.*

'Nemo' is the Latin for 'no one'

Appendix:
Guide to Further Reading

Compiled with the assistance of, and notes from, Patricia Neal.

Witchcraft is difficult to study solely by means of the printed word. One cause of this difficulty is the long-honoured oral tradition of the Craft. The following authors and their books reveal the diversity of witchcraft and its many traditions, but the lack of printed materials prevents the mention of many fine and wise paths. A number of books and articles have been omitted because they are desperately difficult to find. The following list is intended to help the reader new to witchcraft to find out more about it without spending a great deal of money.

To readers who already have some knowledge of witchcraft or who are of a scholarly turn of mind, I recommend also the following two books:

• Selena Fox, *Circle Guide to Wicca and Pagan Resources* (Circle Publications, Madison, Wisconsin). This guide is inexpensive and contains a detailed bibliography as well as lists of periodicals, contacts and suppliers of materials.

• J. Gordon Melton, *Magic, Witchcraft and Paganism in America: A Bibliography* (Garland, New York, 1981.) This bibliography gives an overview of the magical community in the USA from its colonial beginnings to current times. Introductory essays enhance the work's usefulness. This publication is, however, more expensive than *The Circle Guide*.

There are many other books that the serious student of witchcraft will enjoy, but some of these are difficult to find, and frequently gems of information are to be found embedded in dull, scholarly tomes. Folklore, archaeology and mythology resources often provide important information, and some old children's books and books of social history can be valuable. The following two books, for example, though not concerned directly with witchcraft, provide interesting material:

E. Estyn Evans, *Irish Folkways* (Routledge & Kegan Paul, London, 1957)

Michael Dames, *The Silbury Treasure* (1978) and *The Avebury Cycle* (1977). (Thames & Hudson, London).

The various volumes of the series *The Folklore of the British Isles* (general edition Venetia J. Newall; B.T. Batsford, London) are absolutely fascinating.

Almost all histories of witchcraft deal largely with the allegations of the witch-hunters during the centuries of persecution and present quantities of largely dictated confessions made by so-called witches under torture, so they cannot be recommended save as aids to understanding the obsessions, fantasies and paranoia of the witch-hunters. A valuable corrective to these histories can be found on pp. 308-12 of Paul Johnson's fascinating and brilliantly written *A History of Christianity* (Penguin Books, 1980). Succinctly and lucidly, he explains the sociological, political and theological causes of what witches refer to as 'the burning times'.

A thoroughly scholarly account of the centuries of witchcraft persecution, and of what the author calls 'the foulest crime and deepest shame of western civilization', is given in Rossel Hope Robbins' *The Encyclopaedia of Witchcraft and Demonology* (Newnes, London, 1984; Crown Publishers New York). This is widely recognized as the standard work on the subject.

'The burning times' are now over in almost all the world. Persecution, does however, continue. Witches who make no secret of their beliefs have their windows broken and suffer harassment in some communities. I hope that this book and these other books I recommend may do something to remove the misunderstandings and superstitious fears that cause such things to occur.

A Book of Pagan Rituals (Robert Hale, London, 1988; Samuel Weiser; York Beach, Maine, 1978) contains rituals for holidays, initiations etc; it can also serve as a resource for creating new rites.

Margot Adler, *Drawing Down the Moon* (Beacon Press, Boston, 1979). An excellent source book for an overview of the neo-pagan community, mainly in the United States. Not a lot of information is included about the quieter traditional witches.

Charles Bowness, *The Witch's Gospel* (Robert Hale, London, 1979). A chatty, rather lightweight book, which does, however, include some lore not easily found elsewhere.

Raymond Buckland, *Ancient and Modern Witchcraft* (H.C. Publications, New York, 1970). By the same author: *A Pocket Guide to the Supernatural*, (Tandem, London, 1970); *Witchcraft, The Religion*; *Witchcraft from the Inside* (Llewellyn, St Paul, MN, 1971); *Practical Candleburning: Here is the Occult* (Llewellyn, St Paul, MN, 1971); *The Tree: Complete Book of Saxon Witchcraft* (Llewellyn, St Paul, MN, 1984). Seax Wicca (Saxon Witchcraft) as practised by Buckland is outlined in several of these books. His general guides are full of interesting facts and opinions on many occult subjects.

Z. Budapest, *The Holy Book of Women's Mysteries* (Wingbow Press, California, 1989). By the same author: *The Feminist Book of Lights and Shadows*. Strongly feminist Wicca perspectives are found in both works. Poems and interesting 'special rites' are included. Ms Budapest and her circle run an occult supply shop in Southern California and are involved in many networks of occult communities.

Ly Warren Clarke, *The Way of the Goddess* (Prism Press, Bridport, U.K. 1987). This contains much information about kabbalistic and numerological work, and also a rite of self-initiation.

Patricia Crowther, *Lid Off the Cauldron* (Frederick Miller, London, 1981). By the same author: *The Witches Speak* (Athol, Isle of Man, 1965); *Witch Blood!*; *The Secrets of Ancient Witchcraft* (Citadel, Secaucus, NJ, 1988) *Witchcraft in Yorkshire*. Crowther's perspective is Gardnerian. Information is given for planetary rites (common in some but not all traditions), runes and other rites. A most informative book.

Arthur Evans, *Witchcraft and the Gay Counterculture* (Fag Rag Books, Boston, 1978). The only easily available book on witchcraft from the point of view of the gay practitioner. It focuses more on gayness throughout history than on witchcraft but is valuable.

Stewart and Janet Farrar, *A Witch's Bible: Volume I, The Sabbats; Volume II, The Rituals* (Magickal Childe Publishing Co, New York, 1984). This work is a paperback reprint of two earlier books published in Britain by Robert Hale as *Eight Sabbats for Witches* (1981) and *The Witches' Way* (1984). This includes a full account of the Gardnerian Book of Shadows and is valuable as a resource for ritual information.

G.B. Gardner, *The Meaning of Witchcraft* (Aquarian, London, 1970; Samuel Weiser; York Beach, Maine, 1976). By the same author: *Witchcraft Today* (Arrow, London, 1970); *High Magics Aid* (novel) (Houghton, London, 1949). Gardner was one of the first of the modern writers on witchcraft who was also a practitioner. Much of the information found in his books must be read with his ground-breaking role in mind. He initiated both Patricia Crowther (see above) and Doreen Valiente (see below). More information about this interesting man may be found in books by both Crowther and Valiente.

Robert Graves, *The White Goddess: A Historical Grammar of Poetic Myth* (Faber & Faber, London, 1979. Farrar, Straus & Giroux, New York). There is more beauty here, and the answers to more riddles of witchcraft, than in most other modern readily available books on the subject. However, do not look for linear organization: it does not exist!

Paul Huson, *Mastering Witchcraft, A Practical Guide for Witches, Warlocks, and Covens* (Corgi, London, 1972; G.P. Putnam's Sons, New York, 1970). Some fascinating information and some old traditional charms, such as the Anglo-Saxon 'Nine Herbs Charm' are to be found here. Some material is in doubtful taste, but there is a good deal of tongue-in-cheek humour, and the book is definitely worth reading.

Sybil Leek, *Diary of a Witch* (Frewin, London, 1975). A fine journalist in her own right, Mrs Leek wrote many books on witchcraft in a light, easy-reading style that does not intimidate. There are many interesting anecdotes and delightful bits of information that are both useful and amusing. Her training took place in Britain, where she lived much of her life; in her later years she took up residence in the USA, where she passed over to the other side not so many years ago.

Charles G. Leland, *Aradia, or the Gospel of the Witches* (Daniel, London, 1974; Samuel Weiser, York Beach, Maine, 1974). This book, first published in 1899, contains many spells and prayers and presents a traditional Italian witchcraft that has been influenced by religious persecution.

T.C. Lethbridge, *Witches* (Routledge & Kegan Paul, London, 1962; Citadel Press, New York, 1962). An archaeologist's exploration and discussion of the religion of the Mother Goddess from Palaeolithic times to the Middle Ages.

Margaret Murray, *The God of the Witches* (Oxford University Press, 1970). By the same author: *The Witch Cult in Western Europe* (Clarendon, Oxford, 1962). A scholarly treatment of the early history and roots of European witchcraft. A groundbreaking work of its time.

Jeffrey B. Russell, *A History of Witchcraft* (Thames & Hudson, London, 1980). A very readable, well-illustrated history of witchcraft from ancient times to the present day, this is the most sensible current work on the subject. There will be some disagreement about the origins of the Old Religion as presented here, and the distinction between witchcraft and occultism is not made clearly. It is, however, worth attention.

Robin Skelton, *Spellcraft*. (Routledge & Kegan Paul, London, 1978; Sono Nis Press, Victoria B.C.). Subtitled 'A handbook of invocations, blessings, protections, healing spells, love spells, binding and bidding', this book contains examples of verbal magic from many cultures and many periods, as well as instructions on how to cast spells. By the same author: *Talismanic Magic* (Samuel Weiser, York Beach, Maine, 1985). This book surveys all the various kinds of talismans and gives some instructions on how to create and use them.

Robin Skelton and Jean Kozokari, *A Gathering of Ghosts* (Western Producer Prairie Books 1989). The authors describe the different kinds of ghosts and give first-hand accounts of dealing with them. A full rite of exorcism is given in accordance with witchcraft beliefs and procedures.

Starhawk, *The Spiral Dance: A Rebirth of the Ancient Religion of the
Great Goddess* (Harper & Row; San Francisco, 1979). By the
same author: *Dreaming the Dark* (Beacon, Boston, 1983). Inte-
gration of witchcraft into today's world, and its social and
political issues are the keynote in much of Starhawk's work.
She writes in a very inspiring way, and there is much value
in what she has to impart. There are differing schools of
thought among witchcraft communities as to whether or not
politics should enter into witchcraft workings. Starhawk
presents a pro-politics perspective well.

Merlin Stone, *Ancient Mirrors of Womenhood* (two volumes, New
Sibylline Books, New York, 1979). By the same author: *When
God was a Woman* (Harcourt Brace Jovanovich, New York,
1978). Short essays on goddesses worldwide, as well as
goddess worship/witchcraft information can be found here;
a valuable feminist perspective.

Doreen Valiente, *Witchcraft for Tomorrow* (Robert Hale, London,
1978, St Martin's Press, New York, 1978). By the same author:
An ABC of Witchcraft (Robert Hale, London, 1973); *Natural
Magic* (Robert Hale, London, 1975); *Where Witchcraft Lives*.
All of Valiente's books reflect her fine sense of folklore and
her witchcraft knowledge. Although she does not speak for
all, her voice is a valuable one. Her lineage is Gardnerian.
Both *Natural Magic* and *An ABC* have wonderful ideas and
interesting bits of lore not easily found elsewhere. Perhaps
her most indispensable book is *The Rebirth of Witchcraft*
(Robert Hale, London, 1989) in which she gives a detailed
and candid account of the Witchcraft movement in the last
half century and corrects many misconceptions, while also
recounting a number of fascinating experiences, and giving
her own viewpoint on many notable people and various
traditions.

Barbara G. Walker. *The Woman's Encyclopedia of Myths and Secrets*
(Harper & Row, San Francisco, 1983) This thoroughly re-
searched book of over eleven hundred pages contains a
wealth of information about the goddess and goddess worship. By the same author: *The Woman's Dictionary of Symbols
and Sacred Objects* (Harper & Row, San Francisco, 1988). A
useful book for those interested in the subject.

Index

Free Catalog
of New Age & Occult Books From Carol Publishing Group

For over 30 years, the Citadel Library of the Mystic Arts has been hailed as America's definitive line of works on Wicca and White Magic, Occult Sciences and Personalities, Demonology, Spiritism, Mysticism, Natural Health, Psychic Sciences, Witchcraft, Metaphysics, and Esoterica.

Selected titles include: • The Alexander Technique • Amulets and Talismans • Apparitions and Survival of Death • Astral Projection • At the Heart of Darkness • The Bedside Book of Death • Beyond the Light • The Book of Ceremonial Magic • The Book of Spells, Hexes, and Curses • The Book of the Dead • Buddha and the Gospel of Buddhism • Candlelight Spells • The Candle Magick Workbook • The Case for Reincarnation • Classic Vampire Stories • The Complete Guide to Alternative Cancer Therapies • The Concise Lexicon of the Occult • Cosmic Consciousness • Daily Meditations for Dieters • Deceptions and Myths of the Bible • The Dictionary of Astrology • Dracula Book of Great Horror Stories • Egyptian Magic • Egyptian Religion • An Encyclopedia of Occultism • Encyclopedia of Signs, Omens and Superstitions • The Fairy-Faith in Celtic Countries • From Elsewhere • Future Memory • The Grim Reaper's Book of Days • Gypsy Sorcery and Fortune Telling • A History of Secret Societies • The History of Witchcraft • The Hollow Earth • The Holy Kabbalah • How to Improve Your Psychic Power • How to Interpret Your Dreams From A - Z • How To Make Amulets, Charms and Talismans • Hypnosis • The Kabbalah • Know Your Body Clock • The Lost Language of Symbolism, Vols. 1 & 2 • The Magick of Candle Burning • The Magus • Meaning in Dreams and Dreaming • The Modern Witch's Book of Home Remedies • The Modern Witch's Dreambook • The Modern Witch's Spellbook, 1 & 2 • Moon Madness • Not of This World • Numerology • Our Earth, Our Cure • Out-of-the-Body Experiences • The Pictorial Key to the Tarot • The Practice of Witchcraft Today • Principles of Light and Color • The Roots of Healing • Satanism • Satanism and Witchcraft • The Secrets of Ancient Witchcraft • The Secrets of Love Magick • Shouting at the Wolf • Silent Witness • Stranger Than Science • Strangest of All • Strange World • Study and Practice of Astral Projection • The Symbolism of Color • The Talisman Magick Workbook • Tarot Cards • Teachings of Tibetan Yoga • A Treasury of Witchcraft • The Vampire • The Werewolf of Paris • What Happens When You Die • Where the Ghosts Are • The Wicca Book of Days • Wicca Craft • Wicca Spellbook • Window To the Past • Witchcraft • Witchcraft, Sorcery, and Superstition • You Are All Sanpaku • Zen Macrobiotic Cooking

Ask for these New Age and Occult books at your bookstore. To order direct or to request a brochure, call 1-800-447-BOOK or send your name and address to Carol Publishing Group, 120 Enterprise Avenue, Dept 1674, Secaucus, NJ 07094.

Books subject to availability